LAST MAN RIDING

Too many dead men, too many posses, too many bullet wounds — so Brett McCabe decided to quit Tad Ripley's wild bunch. It should have been easy: Ripley was headed for certain death at the hands of Hank Bolan's posse. But, one good deed by McCabe nearly made it impossible. And, as always, the only way to settle things was in gun-smoke . . .

CLAYTON NASH

LAST MAN
RIDING

Complete and Unabridged

LINFORD
Leicester

First published in Great Britain in 2008 by
Robert Hale Limited
London

WORCESTERSHIRE COUNTY COUNCIL	
TW (signature)	039
ULVERSCROFT	14.7.09
W	£8.99
DR	

British Library CIP Data

Nash, Clayton.
    Last man riding- -(Linford western library)
    1. Western stories.
    2. Large type books.
    I. Title II. Series
    823.9'2–dc22

    ISBN 978–1–84782–738–8

Published by
F. A. Thorpe (Publishing)
Anstey, Leicestershire

Set by Words & Graphics Ltd.
Anstey, Leicestershire
Printed and bound in Great Britain by
T. J. International Ltd., Padstow, Cornwall

This book is printed on acid-free paper

1

Badlands

He came over the unfamiliar range by way of a high pass that cut deeply through the walls of grey and black granite.

It was rougher than a cob wall and he dismounted twice, leading the weary brown, clattering over wind-sculpted rocks that could easily cause the horse to break a leg — or cause *him* to. He dropped down into the half-naked foothills and rested a spell, smoking a thin cigarette; the flakes still remaining in the linen sack were meagre and the next smoke would be more wheat straw paper than tobacco.

There were plains, canyons and what looked like another pass where the range curved into a giant horseshoe.

It seemed safe enough, no really good

places for an ambush — at least not from this angle — but he looked back to the towering granite he'd just descended. Maybe he should have paused up there, long enough to watch for a dust cloud, see how far they were behind him . . . Bolan and his damn posse.

To hell with that: however 'far', it would still be too damn close.

Restless, taking no more chances now, he mounted, still smoking, and set out towards that distant pass.

★   ★   ★

He made it through a wide-angle-walled slash between the sandstone, and spotted a splash of green in the distance, at the foot of a hogback rise. It looked mighty lonely and beckoning, way ahead. *God, he might even make it!*

The brown sensed the possibility of feed and water; and he felt the muscles under him working eagerly as he rode towards the hogback. Before he was halfway he felt the touch of a cool wind and welcomed it. Those badlands back beyond the granite range had been a slice of hell with lung-rasping alkali thrown in for good measure.

The only compensation was that they wouldn't figure he would risk such a crossing; Bolan had been right about that. Then he modified that: the posse might come to the same conclusion, but Ripley was a chance-taker, too. If he had survived the ambush he and any others who hadn't been cut down might chance the badlands. Then there was always Bolan — *always!* Who could figure what *he* would do?

But at the waterhole that he found on the hogback amongst some wild, straggly brush it didn't seem like such a worry. He was far ahead of anyone: *he was damned sure of it!*

After bathing the rawhide burns on his wrists, he patted the brown with real affection. Canteen full, belly sloshing, he gnawed one of his last strips of jerky after wiping a thin coating of green from it, and mounted again. The horse didn't want to leave, but he couldn't let it take on any more water. Despite his recent optimism, he might still have to call upon it to make an all-out effort to stay ahead of the dust cloud that would inevitably appear.

The brown had had enough. It resisted him, the whites of its eyes showing. He had never seen this horse act like it before. The right foreleg seemed to lack strength, bent too easily, almost throwing him from the saddle. There were strange noises coming out of that deep chest — and a spray of mucus and froth from the flaring nostrils.

His heart leapt wildly: he had seen *this* before — a horse snake-bit, the poison surging through the weary body.

He had been burying his head in the waterhole when he heard the brown give a wild-sounding whicker, but he had thought it was merely exuberance after so long travelling over waterless badlands, and sloshed more water over his face.

'Goddamn, I should've checked!'

He dismounted. Soothing the wild-eyed, trembling animal, he managed to get a look at the foreleg. There were multiple bites, at least three: deep, bleeding fang-marks, the spread between them telling him it had been a large snake, a brush rattler most likely, but the species hardly mattered. He would never be able to work on those wounds; all he could do was cut them, or at any rate make them bleed more, but the venom was already circulating. Even as he thought this, the horse reared and slashed at him with its hoofs. He rolled aside, came up on all fours, palming up his six-gun. *There was no choice now.* But a gun-shot out here would slap and travel for miles . . .

Still, he owed this horse his life; all he could do now was to put it out of approaching misery and agonizing death. It was already doomed and he could no longer steady it by the trailing reins. If he tried to get close enough to use his knife on the jugular, he would either be bitten or stomped on. The horse didn't know what it was doing by now.

It recognized his moving shape only as an enemy now. The horse lunged. He stepped aside, rammed the gun muzzle under the right ear and dropped hammer. The shot punched the brown's head around and the body twisted, the rump catching him as it fell, knocking him sprawling.

The horse was down, quivering its last. The gunshot had been muffled against the sweaty hide, but the recoil had jarred his wrist.

Now he was afoot, with thunderheads building over the distant granite range and nothing before him but a long stretch of more inhospitable flats.

After reloading the six-gun, he set about stripping the dead horse of the riding gear. Not that there was much in the saddle-bags — not much to sustain him across the waiting miles. But the canteen was full, rain seemed likely and he knew from past experience that a man could live longer without food than he could without water.

Anyway, rain would wipe out his tracks.

★ ★ ★

The rain was heavy when it came, with lightning and thunder. But these had diminished somewhat with the passing of day into night.

His saddle was riding his shoulders, giving him little if any protection from the rain. Before long he would have to lower it and drag it through the mud.

It had been a long, wearying, slogging walk and he knew he had to reach high ground before he dare stop; the heavens had opened and the prospect of forty days and forty nights of deluge didn't seem all that impossible to him at the moment. Already there were a couple of pounds of mud clinging to each boot and splattered over his lower legs, so that he dragged them rather than walking normally.

The slope rose gradually, slippery until he veered left, when, in a flash of lightning that briefly illuminated a couple of hundred acres of sky, he glimpsed some grass and scrub. It was marginally easier than fighting mud, but by the time he had topped the first low rise he had to drop the saddle and flop down on it, water streaming from his sodden hat-brim, chest heaving. The old torn poncho barely fulfilled its purpose of keeping him tolerably dry.

A smoke and a cup of hot coffee, in that order, would go down well, but he had neither, so he put all thought of them out of his mind. He let his gaze wander through the flash-lit darkness, waited for the rumble of distant thunder. He could see brush waving in the wind, a dark bulk that was the rising land and . . . he stiffened.

A light!

Way out here? On a night like this? What the hell kind of campfire or storm lantern could stay burning in this downpour and shrieking wind.

Maybe it was only something reflecting the flare of intermittent lightning . . . ?

That was a stupid thought. He stood up, Not wasting any more time after seeing that the light was still there in the same place, he checked his six-gun, dry beneath the poncho, carefully shielding it from the rain as he did so. The rifle in the saddle scabbard was thoroughly wet despite his having wrapped his spare shirt around it. So, if he was walking into trouble, he would have to depend on the Colt.

To the left, and fifty yards across and up the slope, he saw why the light still shone steadily despite the rain. It was coming from inside a shallow cave: a small campfire. He slid a hand inside the poncho as he saw that there were three men in there. Two were beating the living daylights out of the third.

The man against the wall was very bloody, his quality clothing torn as well as bloodstained. His fair hair was shorter than most men wore it out here, several strands lank with his blood. One of the tormentors was holding the man upright by one shoulder while he pounded on the gory face with his other fist. The third man stood back a little, seemed to be catching his breath, no doubt after having his turn at beating the fair-haired victim.

The breathless man, dressed in worn trail-stained range clothes like his pard, suddenly reached for his hoistered Colt.

'Stand back, Wes! This ain't gettin' us nowhere. My hands hurt an' I ain't got no more . . . breath.'

Wes, still holding the victim against the wall, frowned; he had large features and a drooping moustache.

'The hell you gonna do? Kill the son of a bitch? We'll never find his money that way, Tom. Use your head!'

'I am. See how long he holds out with a slug through his foot — or a kneecap blowed off.'

Wes frowned and apparently eased off his grip on the battered man, for the latter's legs gave way and he fell to his knees, head hanging, blood dripping on to the scuffed earth of the cave floor. Then he sat back, gasping.

Wes grinned, showing scummed, broken teeth. 'Hey, that's a good idea!' he said, reaching for his own Colt.

'I bags first shot! Was my notion!'

'That's OK — he's got two feet, two kneecaps!'

They laughed briefly and Tom spread his muddy boots. 'Move his legs apart — more fun doin' one at a time.'

'You sure are feelin' mean tonight, Tom, ol' son!' Wes moved towards the semi-conscious man who was moaning against the base of the wall.

'Leave him be.'

The rider stepped out of the darkness, dumping his saddle, poncho pushed back so his Colt was clear to draw.

The startled robbers jumped around towards the cave entrance, glimpsed the dark poncho-clad shape. Tom swore, his heart hammering, and brought up his six-gun.

The rider's gun blasted and knocked him halfway across the cave where, he tripped over something on the floor and fell, writhing. Wes's gun came up but a bullet took him in the throat and he dropped, blood hosing the rock wall above the slumped body of the staring, battered victim.

The man had his eyes open now, one swollen so that it was likely he couldn't see much out of it, and he struggled to push himself to a sitting position. The rider ignored him, walked across to where Tom was trying to grip his Colt in both hands, the wavering gun pointing in the general direction of the injured man.

The second bullet took him in the chest and knocked him flat.

The smoking pistol was fully loaded again before the man knelt beside the bleeding victim who was looking up at him with some apprehension.

'Relax, pardner. They sure put the boot to you pretty good. How do you feel?'

'Like — like a horse — trampled me.' The words had a kind of 'polish' to them, not the usual rangeland twang.

He lay there while the rider's hands probed his body and bloody face with surprising gentleness. 'Nothing too important busted, far as I can tell. Couple ribs, I'd guess. You're gonna have a mighty sore belly for a while, too — bruises are already spreading. You know those two?'

The man shook his head, spat some blood and wiped a swollen wrist across his smashed mouth. 'I — I'm Charles Lindeen. I'm on a cattle-buying trip. Those two jumped me in Carson Springs — brought me here. Fools thought I — carried the money — on me.'

The kneeling man arched his eyebrows.

Lindeen attempted a smile, gave up. 'I work with — bank drafts — letters of credit — know better than to carry a lot of cash . . . All those two got was about twenty dollars.' Pain-filled eyes lifted to

13

the rider's face — or what could be seen of it in the light of the campfire which was burning down now.

It was a narrow face, the kind often called 'hawklike' or 'wolfish', the jaw solid, grey eyes either side of a narrow nose, the rest of the features more or less hidden under a few days' dark stubble. Wet hair showing beneath the sodden hat looked to be brownish. He was in his late twenties, or maybe just into his thirties. Tough-looking, hard-muscled.

'To — whom am I — indebted, sir?'

The rider looked kind of startled and smiled thinly.

'That 'whom' kinda brands you as a greenhorn, Mr Lindeen. I've heard of you. Got a big ranch someplace, haven't you? Cattle baron?'

Lindeen chuckled. 'Hardly that — yet!' Then a coughing fit gripped him. He grabbed at his ribs and lay back exhausted, spitting blood, and tried to apologize for the unavoidable gesture. 'Sorry — filthy thing — to do.'

'Forget that kinda eyewash, you need a sawbones. One of those busted ribs is likely to pierce a lung.'

'We — we're a long way from Carson . . . Springs.'

A slight frown showing between his eyes, the rider nodded slowly. 'There's an Overland Line swing-station at Fossil Ridge. You could pick up a stage into Carson from there when you feel up to it.'

'Man — that — that's almost as far as going direct to Carson Springs!' Lindeen was gasping from his protesting outburst, holding his side, watching the other man who, he realized hadn't yet given his name.

Then it came to him: this man didn't want to go anywhere near a town. Because of the law? 'I think — you probably have a — sound suggestion about the stage.'

'I'll strap you up best I can, but the ride there'll be rough on you. You ready for it?'

Lindeen nodded, watching the rider

searching the cave and the gear of the dead men for something that could be used to immobilize Lindeen's ribcage.

He was surprised to see him go through the pockets of the men he had killed and take what little money they held.

'Spoils to the — victor?' Lindeen gasped before he could stop himself.

The man looked at him sharply, said nothing.

'Broke?' Lindeen asked and the silent glance told him he was right. 'They didn't hear you ride up.'

'Horse got snakebit, back a ways. These two won't be needing their broncs. Where are they, by the by?'

'Tethered outside. You — you're quite right. You're entitled to their — belongings. By right of conquest. I suppose.' He tried that smile again, just as unsuccessfully as the first time. 'I have money — not here but I can get it in Carson Springs — and I'd be only too happy to — reward you for all your help.'

'I'm not going to Carson Springs.'

Lindeen nodded gently as the man came back with a coil of rope and a couple of old shirts taken from the warbags of the dead men.

'I'll strap you up and get you to the swing-station. Then you're on your own.'

'I'm — beholden to you, Mr . . . ?'

The grey eyes rested on Lindeen briefly.

The cattleman returned the gaze with his one good eye and nodded slowly. 'Of course. I'll just think of you as — as the Night Rider — who walked!'

The other's thinnish lips stretched out in a brief smile. 'And still has a long way to go.' After a pause he added, 'If you feel the need, call me Brett.'

2

Rolled

It had been a long, hard ride from Telford, and most of the deputies wished they had been out of town when Sheriff Hank Bolan had rigged that ambush at the Express office.

Typical Hank, though. Drag men away from their normal jobs, swear them in temporarily. That way he only had to pay them for the time they spent trying to run down fugitives instead of keeping them on the payroll as 'permanents'.

Hank was tight with a dollar, but he was a good sheriff, put his life on the line time and again for the town. He could probably rely on the townsfolk taking up a decent collection for him when he did retire, but as with a lot of things, Hank Bolan didn't take chances.

Like now, when they finally closed in on the fugitives' temporary camp. Bolan had gathered them in a group up on the ridge, in the dark of clustered timber, and laid it out straight from the shoulder.

'Any man here stumbles, drops his gun, cocks it when we're close enough to alert them varmints, answers to me.' He glared around, not elaborating — not even *having* to — they all knew the sheriff's mean streak.

The heavy rain thundering down right now would help with the attack. It swished through the woods and foot-hills here to the north of the badlands like a flapping curtain, blown by the wind. It rattled on their ponchos and they swore as Bolan snapped, setting the example: 'Get 'em off.'

'Judas priest! If a bullet don't nail a man, goddamn pneumonia will,' some-one bitched.

'*I'll* get you before any damn pneumonia if you don't shuck that slicker pronto!'

It was done and they shivered and muttered curses, but used their bodies to protect their guns for one last check. Bolan himself thumbed three cartridges into his new pump-action shotgun, moving the slide carefully so its metallic whisper couldn't possibly disturb the men sleeping in the three bedrolls just visible beyond the glow of the dying fire: a flat-rock shelter had been rigged but it wasn't effective and the coals spat and sizzled.

Then the sheriff straightened in his saddle. 'Where the hell's the fourth man?' he hissed. 'Four got away.'

'Three'll do me, if we're goin' in there,' a second deputy allowed and there were murmurs of agreement: these robbers had already demonstrated their ruthlessness back on the streets of Telford.

'We go in shootin'!' Bolan snapped. 'If someone's gonna get killed, it ain't gonna be us — get it?'

Take no prisoners, in other words.

'But I want Ripley alive,' the lawman

added harshly. 'There's a slew of money to recover.'

The campfire was dying rapidly and, impatient now, Bolan lifted the shotgun and heeled his mount forward, starting down the slippery slope — and then guns opened up from below: *the bedrolls were decoys*.

Bullets whistled and thunked and leaves and twigs rained down around the lawmen. Someone yelled, but it sounded more like with fright than pain.

The sheriff pumped his shotgun slide, blasting off all three rounds one after the other, but so close together it sounded like a rolling thunderclap.

Below, a man cried out — *that* was pain! Bolan grinned tightly as he reloaded, fumbling, but getting the job done swiftly. Rifles cracked around him and were answered from the fugitives' cover below. The gunflashes were the only targets: the outlaws stayed well hidden.

'You sure that fourth sonova ain't

down there, Hank?'

'Ride on down and get in amongst 'em! We'll count heads later.'

Right now, no one was keen to lead the charge down the slope, so Bolan set the example with a rebel yell loud enough to be heard above the wind-driven rain.

The others followed, lying low on their mounts as lead whined over their heads. Two horses went down thrashing, their riders briefly airborne, before they landed in swaying brush. Other men veered away, racing for cover.

Bolan found himself out in front — alone. Then, even as he turned to harangue the bullet-dodging deputies, his mount seemed to run into an invisible wall. He sailed over the horse's head, and man and beast hit the ground together, sliding and slithering.

Desperation move: shoot the horses, leave the posse afoot . . . .'Damn you, Ripley!'

Shaken, ears roaring, Bolan heard the outlaw mounts taking off across the slope. Hoarsely, he yelled for back-up and a couple of posse men rode up warily, spurring into the dark of the predawn. Others came out of cover to follow.

On his feet by now, Bolan yanked one man out of the saddle as he rode past, left the rider tumbling, and swung on board. He had lost the shotgun in his fall and didn't take time to look for it now, just raked with his spurs.

The three outlaws led them on one hell of a chase through the trees, over a brush-clad rise, which suddenly threw them into open country. There was enough light now for them to see their only chance: a buffalo wallow, half-filled with muddy water.

They splashed into it, their mounts rearing and plunging. It was almost waist-deep and they waded to the sloping sides, hoping their guns weren't too drowned to fire.

Bolan spread his men in a short arc, sending two around the wallow to take up a position where they would be able to pick off the outlaws if they tried to get out on that side.

'Give up, Ripley! We got you pinned. Stay put and we'll shoot you like fish in a barrel. Try to run and we'll nail you even easier. What'll it be?'

'I ain't gonna look at the lousy world through a set of iron bars for the rest of my life, Bolan! Hell with you!'

'That your last word? I hope!'

'Last you'll ever hear — from me or anyone else!'

A man's head suddenly appeared over the edge of the wallow, taking them by surprise as its owner threw a rifle to his shoulder and triggered two swift shots. Bolan was thrown back over his mount's rump to sprawl in the mud. The horse shuddered, knelt down almost daintily, then spilled on to its side, pinning the lawman.

'Get it — *off me*!' There was blood on the sheriff's face, and his poncho was torn up around his neck. 'My goddamn leg's — broken!'

Two men ran to him, watching the

wallow warily. But the posse men were good and mad now and peppered the crater's edge with dozens of bullets.

The wounded Bolan was dragged out unceremoniously from under the dying horse, pale but plenty riled, too.

'Don't worry, Hank. Them bastards down there can't get away.'

'They — better — not! An' — watch for that — that fourth man . . . I don' want any of 'em gettin' away.' Bolan gasped and passed out.

★ ★ ★

As he swung through the partly open door of the boxcar, Brett McCabe knew it was a mistake. They were waiting for him, must have seen him win that last poker hand in the smoke-choked back room of the shanty saloon at Ryker's Outpost.

He had left the card-table with bulging pockets, surprised the pot had been so big in such a dirtwater settlement. He cursed himself now for being greedy: he should have been content with selling the broncs he had taken from the two men he had killed in the cave.

Now, while he was still off-balance from his leap through the conveniently open door, four shadows detached themselves from the deeper shadows of the boxcar and advanced towards him. There was no time to reach for his gun as he fought for balance. They were upon him and he recognized the first man, the one with the Vandyck beard and who smelled strongly of bay rum. He had been among the onlookers during the last hand of the game and had whistled loudly when Brett had taken the pot with an ace-high straight. Now he and his coyotes were going to take it from him.

If they could.

They had set him up by jamming the car's sliding door part-way open, making it easy to choose. Now the Vandyck lunged at Brett as he swayed in the opening. He parried the first blow, sank a fist into the man's midriff, lifted a knee and hooked an elbow behind the head. The man's screams as he hurtled through the doorway echoed through the boxcar, gave the others pause — but only briefly.

They rushed him — and Brett confused them by rushing to meet them. Startled, they slowed, but by then Brett was in amongst them, fists and elbows and knees, hooking and jabbing, boots raking a leg that had one man sobbing a curse through his pain. He stumbled as the train gathered speed on the downgrade.

The next man within range was shorter than Brett but wide as a barn door, crouching, hands like hams jabbing at his face. Brett yanked his head aside, got in one solid punch and, as the squat man rocked back, he head-butted him.

The nose was squashed and blood flooded over the man's jutting jaw. His eyes momentarily crossed and he clawed at the wall for support. Brett drove a hammerblow to the back of his head, smashing his face into the slatted wall.

The other two were only partly recovered but they acted in concert, the one with the raked shins hooking two pile-drivers into Brett's kidneys. Brett's legs buckled and the second man threw his thick arms about him, heaved him violently across the breadth of the boxcar. He hit the plank wall so hard he thought it would splinter. Bouncing off, he stumbled in an effort to keep balance; the train was really moving now, rocking and clattering along the rails.

By then the head-butted squat man had turned, his face a mask of thick blood, smeared teeth bared as he raised one hard-knuckled fist and brought it down, whistling, towards Brett's jaw.

Brett turned his head but the fist skidded along his jawbone. He felt skin tear. Then they were holding his arms while the bloody-faced man wiped the back of a wrist across his smashed mouth. He set his boots for more solid footing.

After that, it wasn't anything Brett cared to remember. It was mostly pain — jarring pain in his body, more pain in the groin as a knee lifted savagely — a clubbing fist on his neck, pain mixed with a deafening roaring in his ears. His legs were too weak to hold him. He sagged, supported by the two thieves while the other man's thick shoulders worked with every hammering punch.

Later, he recalled lying on the filthy floor with its soiled straw and grit and old cow manure, feeling like a horse had kicked in his ribs and stomped on his back. He was only vaguely aware of these things when a kick to his head sent him spinning away into blackness . . .

Panting, dripping blood, the robbers went through his pockets, took every cent he had, and a stag-handled clasp knife that Brett's elder brother, Calvin, had given him before he had gone away to war — from where he had never returned. Brett had treasured that knife all through the long years since that night of parting, the main blade had worn narrow through many sharpenings and much use.

If there had been a choice he'd have rather parted with his winnings than that knife. Now everything had been stolen.

Then they dragged him to the door and kicked him out into the night. He tumbled like a rag doll, struck the slope of bluemetal and flopped and skidded all the way down into the ditch at the bottom, gravel piling up against his body.

3

Wrangler

The last bandage was in place around his torso now and Brett sighed as the nurse tied it off. The doctor was washing his hands in a bowl of cloudy water. He was an ordinary-looking man in his fifties, but he was mostly bald and the remaining side hair stuck out like tufts of wire.

'You're a lucky man, mister. You'll have sore ribs for a few days but those support bandages will help. Headaches will come and go and you may have the occasional dizzy spell. But you're about as tough as any man I've ever doctored.'

'Looks can be deceiving, Doc. I feel mighty — fragile.' Brett nodded his thanks as the nurse cleared away the bloody cloths and used antiseptic swabs. 'Doc, I'm obliged but I can't pay you. They took every cent I had.'

'With that bruise on the side of your head, I wondered if you would remember. You must have a hard head.'

'Solid bone,' Brett allowed bitterly. 'How else can I explain walking into a set-up like that . . . ? No better'n a damn greenhorn.'

The doctor stared at him steadily. 'The sheriff wants to see you. The railroad gang that found you couldn't tell him much. I said I'd send you along to his office after I saw to your injuries.'

His eyes narrowed as he noticed Brett's discomfort although the man covered well — just not quite fast enough for the medic's eagle eye. 'If you're not feeling too chipper you could spend a day or two in my infirmary. I'd see you weren't disturbed until you felt like facing life again.'

He could see Brett was tempted but, after some thought, the man shook his head slowly, lifting one hand to touch the tape above his left eye which it had taken five sutures to close the deep gash there. In a mirror he could see his face was spotted with dabs of yellow iodine and, in two places, red mercurochrome.

He doubted that his own father would have recognized him. He sure didn't resemble any picture that might be on a wanted dodger in the sheriff's possession . . . *He hoped!*

Brett swayed as he stepped down from the bench, grabbed the edge. 'Doc, I owe you enough. Dunno when I'll be able to pay, but I'll do it. Just gimme a bill.'

The sawbones looked at him for a long moment, obviously considering.

'Don't look like that, Doc. I said I'll pay. You might never see me again, but your money'll turn up sometime in the mail.'

The doctor made out a bill and handed it to the injured man, who put it in his shirt pocket. The shirt was an old one that the medic had given him to replace the blood-soiled and torn shirt he had been wearing when he had been brought in.

Brett limped his way into the front office, paused as he saw a creased copy of the *Bensonville Bugle* on a chair. He picked it up, eyes drawn to a column headline partly hidden by the fold in the paper. Opening it out, he saw it fully: TELFORD TRIO JAILED FOR LIFE. In smaller type underneath: *Fourth Robber Dies In Badlands*. He read swiftly, just the first few lines, which gave the names of the three bank robbers: Tad Ripley, Yank Bilby, and Boots Skene . . . Tough luck, boys. *Can't think of anyone more deserving . . .*

He heard the doctor giving instructions to the nurse to fetch something and, as the door handle rattled, he hurriedly dropped the paper and went out on to the boardwalk.

Bensonville was a lot bigger than he had expected. He only knew it was a cowtown, had been a rip-roarer of a trail stop until Sheriff Carl Casmeier had arrived with twin six-shooters and a sawed-off shotgun. Within days the town had had to build a temporary jail to take the overflow of prisoners from the original hoosegow. The local court had never been so busy. Brett didn't know Casmeier but knew his reputation. He wasn't keen to meet the man but what else could he do? Steal a horse to clear town? Well, if he *had* to come face to face with Casmeier, he sure didn't want it *that* way.

He found the lawman behind his large desk in a neat office in the front of the cellblock. A stained-wood fence separated the sheriff's space from the entrance. Casmeier was only about five feet eight inches tall, wouldn't weigh a hundred and twenty pounds. His face was ordinary, though he didn't smile much — if at all — and his head was small, straight black hair combed back in a cowlick. He nodded.

'Come around here and take a decent chair,' the sheriff invited.

Brett was aware that, despite the sheriff's efforts, he wasn't relaxed; he did not feel easy in the presence of this highly respected lawman. *Any* lawman for the matter of that.

'Lucky for you that railroad mainte-nance gang happened along with their hand trolley when they did. You able to fill in the gaps for me?'

It was said casually enough but there was something in Casmeier's grey eyes that told Brett he had *better* give all the details. Those eyes wouldn't miss a thing.

So he spoke slowly, hedging a little, but making out it was because of the kick in the head he had taken.

The sheriff, making notes as Brett talked, glanced up. 'Don't b'lieve I caught your name.'

'Calvin Brett,' he said easily, using his dead brother's name with his own Christian name. Linking 'Brett' with 'McCabe' just might stir Casmeier's memory. Brett figured this dapper lawman with the pomaded hair was not someone to underestimate and hope to get away with it.

'OK, Calvin Brett. You'd recognize

these men who robbed you if you saw them again?'

'I might — but it was pretty damn murky inside that boxcar. Think I'd seen the one I threw off somewhere before.'

The cool green eyes touched his blotched face. 'Railroad would probably like to hear about this. They might even try to stick you for the fare. Don't much care for a man hitching a free ride — 'specially if he's got his pockets full of poker winnings.'

Brett spread his hands. 'I'd figured to ride the rails long before I won the money, Sheriff.'

'But you'd already sold two horses — and maybe I better get some more details about how you come by them.'

Judas priest! This damn lawman came at you from all directions! And he looked so damn — ordinary!

The street door opened then and a man wearing a hip-length corduroy jacket and brown cord trousers hurried in, some papers in one hand, pushing back his curl-brim hat with the other.

'Sheriff, sorry to interrupt, but I need you to OK this booking for the cattle pens — they tell me you're the man to see.' There was a lifting query in the man's words and then he noticed Brett and nodded. 'I beg your pardon, sir, but I have to have these papers signed in time for me to make the train to Rincon — ' He broke off abruptly. 'I know you, don't I? But — your — face . . . '

'Howdy, Mr Lindeen,' Brett said slowly, inwardly cursing the man's arrival at this moment. 'When I'd finished with the sheriff here, I was gonna try to contact you about that job.' *If you want to square with me. Lindeen, now's the time!*

Lindeen frowned slightly. Had he offered Brett a job before they had parted back at the Overland swing-station all those weeks ago . . . ? Well, if he hadn't, he should've. Though it was obvious at the time that Brett was on the run. But he was still obligated to the man.

He flicked his gaze from Brett to the grim-faced sheriff and played his hunch that Brett was in need of a friend. 'Ah, of course. You're Brett!' The cattleman turned to Casmeier. 'Hard to recognize him with all that warpaint on his face. I need more mustangs for my big cattle drive and I asked Big Bill Stedmann from the Gridiron up on the Platte if he could recommend someone reliable.'

'I know Stedmann's reputation,' cut in Casmeier. 'He's thought of right highly all through this neck of the woods.' He swung towards Brett. 'Why didn't you say you worked for Stedmann?'

'I don't. Not now, that is. I — er — accepted Mr Lindeen's offer and was on my way to his place when I ran into that trouble in the boxcar.'

That word, 'trouble', and the side-long glance Brett gave him, sharpened Lindeen's interest. 'Is there something I can do for you, Brett? Any — legal matter that needs straightening out, perhaps?'

Brett shook his head. 'No, thanks. I was rolled in a boxcar by a few hardcases. I didn't get a good look at 'em so they'll likely get away with it.'

'Not all of 'em.' Lindeen and Brett both looked sharply at the small town-tamer. 'We picked up that one with the funny beard wandering beside the track.'

'The Vandyck?' Brett asked, frowning. 'You never said.'

'Just did. He's in the cells. You can identify him, but he's talking his head off. We'll get the others eventually. But Mr Vandyck is on his way to the territorial pen.'

'That was fast and efficient work, Sheriff,' Lindeen opined as Brett heaved stiffly to his feet.

'I've given you all I can recall, Sheriff. I'll take at look at the one in your cells if you want.'

When he returned from the cell block with Casmeier, Brett nodded to Lindeen. 'He's one of 'em all right.'

'I'll need your written statement,' the

sheriff said. 'Including where you got those hosses you sold off — at Kidman Creek, south of Ryker's, wasn't it?'

Brett avoided looking at Lindeen now, hoping the man might help him out here. He couldn't very well tell Casmeier the horses belonged to two men he'd killed in that cave. He didn't want to be placed anywhere near that neck of the woods at that particular time. *Too close to Telford.*

'Couple I caught and saddle-broke,' Brett said, suddenly inspired by Lindeen's mention of him being a 'mustanger'. 'They were still kinda skittish, acting up, slowing me down, and I didn't want to miss out on the job with Mr Lindeen. So I sold 'em, figured to take the train instead.'

The lawman pushed pad and pencil across the desk and gestured for Brett to start writing. 'You can witness his signing the statement, Mr Lindeen. While he's doing it, let's see your papers. Town council built those pens at my suggestion. I saw 'em work for

Dodge and Wichita, convinced this here council that hiring 'em out would bring in a good income. You might notice we have a mighty nice-looking town here: fresh paint, graded streets, deep rainwater gutters, no broken boardwalks. We got us a city hall, brick court house, even an opera house, and a steeple on the church.' He paused, added a little distantly, slightly embarrassed by his enthusiasm, 'All thanks to renting out those holding pens. We keep our fees reasonable.'

'Any fee for use of holding pens has to be seen as just one more expense for a cattleman,' Lindeen said a trifle testily. 'You have us at a disadvantage, of course, Bensonville being the last big railhead in this part of the territory. Here's my personal cheque, Sheriff.'

'You checked these dates with the railroad?' At Lindeen's assurance he had, Casmeier took up a pen and signed saying, 'This is your date limit. You arrive between these dates or you lose your booking.'

'I've hired those pens for two weeks, allowing for delays along the trail! If I arrive anytime during those weeks, before the expiry date, I'm entitled to use the pens for whatever time remains.' Lindeen knew his rights.

Casmeier heaved a sigh. 'Always someone to worry about the 'ifs' and 'buts'. I just told you that. The pens are yours during the time you've booked — and — that — time — only. Not one minute past midnight on the last day on this form.'

He tossed the signed forms across the desk, picked up Brett's brief statement and examined it. After Lindeen signed as witness he placed it in a folder. 'All right, Brett. You can go. But I'd like you to stick around town. You're Mr Lindeen's responsibility now until I say different.'

'Just a minute, Sheriff! I'm quite willing to go to bat for Mr Brett, but I resent you telling me that I *have* to, just on your say-so.'

'Lindeen, we have a tried and true

ordinance in Bensonville. I take my job seriously and I've made this town the envy of many by enforcing that ordinance. We make no exceptions — none. No matter how rich or powerful a visiting cattleman may think he is on his own dunghill. You play by our rules or not at all.' Casmeier actually smiled then, spreading his small hands. 'Simple as that. Good day, gents.'

★　★　★

'You're lucky you never broke a leg when they threw you off the train.'

'Yeah. I was out of it, naturally limp, everything relaxed. That helped.'

Lindeen nodded a trifle absently. 'I've gone out on a limb for you, Brett. Oh, don't worry. I know how obliged I am to you. But once the people at that swing-station got me to a sawbones I got a mite curious about you.'

Brett said nothing, looking out of the window at the passing countryside as the train rolled south on the long haul to Rincon and Stallion Forks in the Hondo Basin.

'There was a town not too far from where you and I met. Telford. Seems there was an Express office robbery around that time. But the sheriff, man named Bolan, was forewarned somehow and rigged an ambush. Two robbers and a townsman were killed. But four got away. With the money.'

He paused but Brett's features were blank.

'Later, Bolan's posse ran down three of the robbers. His posse wounded them all including the leader, a man named Ripley. They all got life sentences on the rockpile in the territorial prison. But there's never been any real sign of the fourth man. Bolan thinks he took a chance in the badlands . . . and they did find a dead horse out there, I hear.'

'He'd have to be mighty desperate to try to cross the badlands . . . or be forced into doing it.'

'That's a curious thing to say. Bolan thinks he probably died out there. The money was never recovered.'

'Believe I heard about that trouble in Telford.'

Lindeen smiled thinly. 'Wondered if you had. Seems none of the trio would tell the law the name of the fourth man. I wonder how he could inspire loyalty in such rabble.'

Brett smothered a snort of derision. 'Ripley likely aims to square things some day. I've heard he's mean enough.'

'Well, that day will be a lonnngg way off — if it ever comes.' Lindeen took out a leather cheroot-case edged in silver and offered it to Brett who took one. He found a vesta in his shirt pocket and lit both cheroots.

'Do you know anything about break-ing in wild horses? I just mentioned mustangs to Casmeier off the top of my head. I noticed at the cave you seemed at home with horses.'

'My father was a wrangler. Me and my brother grew up helping him. You picked it right, tagging me as a mustanger. That's if you still aim to put me on your payroll.'

'I believe in giving a man a chance if I think he deserves it. Just getting you out of Casmeier's hands doesn't even begin to square away what you did for me. I owe you my life.' Lindeen blew smoke, settled his gaze on Brett's battered face. 'I hope Casemeier won't give you any undue . . . trouble?' Brett said nothing. 'You've no idea how pleased I am to see you, Brett. A man like you is just what I need on this drive.'

'Like me?'

'Yes. Tough, knowledgable, reliable . . . '

'Handy with a gun?'

Lindeen smiled. 'That, too. It'll be a long drive.'

Brett watched the monotonous countryside, smoking.

Hiring his gun for a few dollars was nothing new. And this chore would take him a long way from Telford.

The further the better.

4

Chain

Brett had never been to Stallion Forks. All he knew about it was that it was the town centre for the Tularosa Valley, backed by a spur of the San Andres Range called, locally, the Blanco Crestas. The valley was watered by the Rio Hondo, which nurtured succulent grasses unique in that part of the territory, on the flats and in the foothills. It had been settled for ten years or more now.

Lindeen had been one of the lucky ones, arriving early, able to claim, and hold, huge tracts of range. Slowly, patiently, over the years he had worked these up into pastures and gradually filled them with good-quality cattle.

It had called for a lot of outlay, tying up thousands of dollars, but Lindeen apparently had that kind of money and

48

laid the foundations for a cattle empire whose size would one day rival some of the imperial kingdoms of Europe.

He seemed a decent type of man, treated his hired hands well, paid them good wages, even saw they were adequately clothed come winter or the rains. These things made him popular — and sometimes the target for ambitious rustlers. That time in the cave at the edge of the badlands wasn't the first time he had been abducted by men who thought they could beat a lot of dollars out of him.

But he might well have been killed by those two thieves who had been attacking him if Brett McCabe hadn't happened upon them.

Lindeen was genuinely keen to help Brett in any way he could; obviously he suspected — knew, maybe — that Brett was no angel, but that knowledge was overridden by the fact that the man had saved Lindeen's life.

Brett realized that he had had a close shave with Casmeier, was obliged to the cattleman for coming to his aid. As far as he was concerned that, together with Lindeen's settling of the Bensonville sawbones's bill and giving him a job, squared off everything.

He knew damn well Lindeen didn't see it that way and he would have to be on his guard to make sure the cowman didn't get carried away and try to — what was that big word some do-gooder had thrown at him one time down in Laredo? Oh, yeah — as long as Lindeen didn't try to *rehabilitate* him.

At the same time, Brett had had a bellyful of riding the owlhoot trail — still wasn't sure how he had gotten into it in the first place. *Yes, he was, only he didn't like to admit it, even to himself; he had, essentially, volunteered.*

He had been several years younger then, maybe seven or eight: that part didn't matter. The thing was he had discovered that he had a natural speed with a six-gun that left a lot of men breathless and staring once they had seen it demonstrated — and more than a few men dead too.

Riding high, wide and handsome, well, passably good-looking, with full pockets from an unexpected bounty paid him after a provoked gunfight, he had found that there were men who wanted to try him out. Try out his gun speed, that was.

He did his best to avoid it but soon discovered the only way out of such challenges was to accept them and to hell with the consequences. It went against the grain for him, but he felt himself sliding gradually into the 'gunslinger' life whether he liked it or not.

Then came the first offer to *hire* his gun. An agency would pay $200 just to have him escort a payroll through the sierra chain and up to the mines. Eleven miles, which made it just under twenty dollars a mile.

It was easily earned. Two disgruntled mine employees had made their try at robbing the payroll party and he had shot them both. One died of his wounds, the other was hanged by a cold-hearted judge in Bandito Springs a few weeks later.

The trial had meant publicity and more offers came in; dollars for guns — *his* gun. It went along smoothly enough for a time but ultimately it was boring and he cut out halfway through a job, offering to return half the fee, but made an enemy of the man in charge. And when the payroll was robbed on the second half of the journey, this man claimed Brett McCabe had set it up, been involved. Why else would he have quit and made it easy for the robbers?

The slur stuck and the company put out a Wanted dodger on him. Other dodgers appeared; someone using his name had been involved in other robberies and a couple of shoot-outs with dead men left behind on each occasion.

Then, on the run, he had bought into a gunfight that had spilled over into his lonely camp in the hills one night. Two wounded strangers had staggered in, said they were miners who had struck a small bonanza, had been claim-jumped by the men who had shot them, and who were not far behind.

Brett had been tagged as a friend of the wounded men and he had had to shoot it out with the trail-grimed trio who had ridden into the camp, intent on killing their quarry. Brett had killed two, wounded the third who got away. Later — *too* late by then — he found out that they were bounty hunters, semi-official deputies, chasing the wounded two, who were survivors from an express train robbery that had gone wrong. Turned out he knew one man, Tad Ripley, from the war.

But he had been recognized and his Wanted dodger was right up there alongside those of the men he had 'rescued' Tad Ripley and Yank Bilby.

He had been mad at first, then, hounded by posses, the wounded men tagging along, he said to hell with it. He had been getting blamed for all kinds of crimes. Half the time he was on the dodge for something he hadn't done.

So he decided he might as well be on the dodge for something he *had* done — with money in his pockets.

And that was how he became a part of Tad Ripley's wild bunch.

It had been exciting enough, profitable, too, and he had seen a lot of country, crossed a lot of state lines, several times jumped the Rio Grande into Mexico and 'rested up' for a spell. After a while he figured maybe he had been born to ride the owlhoot. He hadn't given it a lot of thought; mostly Ripley's jobs were well-planned and killing wasn't all that frequent. But it did happen. Inevitably.

Was that really how he had rationalized it? he wondered now, sitting up straighter as the train rolled towards the siding at Rincon. Lindeen had told him they would pick up a stage here that would take them across to Stallion Forks where the big trail herd was gathering at his ranch. It was called

Chain, the brand being a curve of five links with a 'C' for Charles and an 'L' for Linden in the end ones.

Strangely, Brett had about made up his mind to make that Telford hold-up his last job, anyway. He was tired of the endless riding, always looking for distant dust clouds that invariably drew closer until the posse men were easy targets; he was tired of dodging bullets, living wild, most of the time with an only partly full belly, feeling the onset of rheumatics from sleeping so much on damp ground. Most of all he was tired of Tad Ripley.

Tad was a boisterous type, full of smiles, but always with teeth gritted; they were not relaxcd, friendly smiles. He was highly suspicious and, essentially, a killer. *No witnesses*, was the style Ripley had developed, and when Mort Damon was blasted by Ripley's shotgun in Telford — needlessly, except to make the ambushers think twice about rushing the gang — well, right then Brett figured that this was where their trails parted.

'Better grab your . . . ' Lindeen stopped, but his words had broken Brett's line of thought. 'I was going to say 'grab your warbag'. Forgot you don't have one. Well, we'll fix that before we catch the stage to Stallion.' He nodded out through the window and Brett realized that the train had slowed considerably while he had been thinking about his past. 'Here's Rincon. We'll be home by this time tomorrow. We'll stay at a hotel tonight, enjoy a decent meal and a few drinks and see what the evening brings.' Lindeen laughed briefly. 'That meet with your approval?'

Brett smiled with his battered mouth moving only slightly.

'Sounds OK to me, but I guess any 'ladies' who have any notion of entertaining us might run a mile when they see this face of mine.'

'Don't worry about that. You'll be surprised at how quickly a handful of dollars can change a woman's mind!'

With a flick of one eyebrow, Lindeen added, 'Change *anyone*'s mind.'

★ ★ ★

There was a delay.

A stage had been held up, two passengers wounded, one dying later. The thieves, Mexicans according to the survivors, burned the stage and turned loose the passengers after robbing them and assaulting one young woman.

The back-up stage was up on blocks, having spokes in the rear wheels renewed after splitting the originals when they hit a washaway because the drunken driver was going way too fast.

Lindeen was edgy, swore as he paced the hotel room. 'Two more days! Goddamnit, these jerkwater stagelines are OK until something goes wrong and then they never have enough back up! By God, I think I'll look into buying out this one; make sure I have a coach when I need one.'

He lit a cheroot with jerky motions,

glared at Brett, who was standing by the window looking out on to the streets of Rincon.

'Well? What d'you think of that idea?'

'OK, if you can afford it, I guess. Won't get us outta here any faster this time, though.'

Lindeen scowled and then, halfway through it, changed it to a crooked smile. 'You're right. I'll still make the date limit, even if I have to push a little harder. It's just that I'm impatient to get back to the basin. Got a lot of arrangements to make yet. We'll find a gunsmith and you can fix yourself up with another Colt and rifle, all right?'

It was all right, though Brett would rather have rested. He was feeling better but knew he still needed to take things easy. But he still had to replace his guns.

'Got to round up and bust a bunch of mustangs before the drive? Or do you have a *remuda* already?'

'Only partly. I don't see how you'll be fit enough to break mustangs, but I can give you some men. You tell 'em what you want done. You won't have to look far for the horses. We know their territory and right now there's a suitable bunch grazing a canyon only a few miles from my line. I've had men stake it out to make sure they stay put till we're ready for 'em.'

The gunsmith had nothing very special. Mostly he just sold standard-issue handguns and rifles, with a few shotguns thrown in. He had a good array of knives, though, and Brett chose a Barlow with stag handles that resembled the one stolen by the attackers in the boxcar.

For a handgun, he picked one of the new Frontier Model Colts, plus a small toolkit in a roll. The gunsmith, tall, lanky, his fingers permanently ingrained with powder and gun oil, winked as he pushed the kit across the counter.

'Aim to do a little work on the Colt?'

Brett nodded. 'A lot if I have to.'

The gunsmith nodded. 'Yeah, straight-from-the-factory stuff's OK for everyday totin' around, but a man like yourself might find some . . . modifications useful. I can sell you a factory manual, with lots of diagrams . . . ?'

Brett shook his head.

'Know the workin's that well, eh?' There was sarcasm there and Brett didn't answer. He stepped across to the ammunition shelves and began taking down cardboard cartons of cartridges.

The gunsmith sighed and began to total up the bill.

Lindeen paid only after scanning it and querying a couple of charges which the flushed gunsmith eventually agreed to drop. He evidently wasn't a fool with his money, just because he had a lot of it . . . which could be how he came by a lot of it in the first place, Brett allowed, as he picked up his weapons in the gunnysack the gunsmith provided.

Lindeen said he would go and arrange for some extra stores to be shipped down to his ranch. Brett went back to the hotel room, unrolled the tool kit and took the big Colt apart. He did some work with a slim, fine file on the trigger sear, using short, light strokes as he examined it by eye, making sure the metal facings were perfectly flat so that they met squarely. He did some more delicate work on the hammer-fall and made some partial modification to the spring, which left his hands and fingers aching afterwards, seeing as he didn't have a small table vice to hold it. The Colt's mechanism was about as good as he could make it. After checking and removing a couple of moulding marks, he reassembled the weapon, smearing oil on meagrely, just enough to make the parts move more smoothly, and so more quickly, but not enough to attract dirt and form a clogging paste. He filed down the blade foresight which stood way too high and was liable to snag the holster. The cedar butt grips were too thick for his liking, so he pared them down with his new clasp knife, afterwards smoothing and shaping the pleasant-smelling wood to his satistfaction.

He was trying his draw from the holster when Lindeen came back. He stopped in the doorway, admiring the economical, sleek movements, the blurring speed of flashing blued-metal.

'Thank God you're on my side!' He closed the door behind him, held up a flat flask of whiskey that had a red bond seal on the cap. 'Who would believe you could find such quality liquor in a place like Rincon? This should help the time pass more pleasantly.'

As he uncapped the bottle and poured two liberal drinks in the hotel water glasses, he watched Brett splash water from the ornate china jug into the matching bowl, then submerge his holster, now free of the cartridge belt.

'What on earth . . . ?'

'Holster was made for my old Colt.' The new model has slightly different lines. When the leather's soaked thoroughly, I'll ram my gun in and leave it overnight. It'll mould itself to the Colt's shape. A little neatsfoot oil and some beeswax dressing and I'll be primed for bear.'

Lindeen looked thoughtful as he handed Brett his drink, lifted his glass in a toasting gesture. 'May you use it in good health — and straight shooting! All on behalf of the Charles Lindeen Cattle Company!'

He grinned. Brett nodded slightly and took a drink, obviously enjoyed it. 'Smooth.'

Lindeen laughed. 'Succinct and precise as usual! You speak with economy, Brett — the way you shoot.'

'Like to make every bullet count.'

'Well, let's hope we don't have to use too many on the big drive.'

'You're coming?' Brett sounded surprised.

'Of course! I may not look it, but I'm a hands-on cattleman, Brett. I built my first ranch house from the ground up, fought off renegade Indians and outlaws who thought my early herds would be easy pickings. I opened up the Big Trail to Socorro, which was as far as the railroad came in those days, Now we only have to cover half the distance to Bensonville. Yes, I'll be trail-bossing the drive.'

Why did he have the notion that that might not be such a good idea as it first sounded, Brett thought as he downed the rest of his whiskey. A rich man keeping an eye on his assets? Or a perfectionist . . . ?

Then he took up the new Winchester rifle and began to unscrew the cover plate over the action; he reached for the roll of tools when it came free.

'There'll be plenty of places for you to practise with your guns once we get back to Chain.'

Brett nodded without looking up.

And he would use those places well, checking his weapons to be sure they were as reliable as he could make them before the drive got under way.

Old habits die hard.

5

Rio Hondo

After the long, jolting stage ride, Brett was glad to see the town called Stallion Forks. Mid-sized, weathered in some parts, neat and tidy in others — those mostly out towards the residential section. There were a few stores lining the main drag, and he could identify at least two saloons.

But there was little time to see much. The stage was met by three cowboys from Chain, the big, black-haired ranny with the jaw like a squared-off boulder being the foreman, Harve Ricketts. He was around forty, his big hands calloused from years of rope burns and manual labour. His grip was hard, harder than necessary, and he looked into Brett's eyes as he squeezed, thick lips moving in a crooked smile.

'Hope I din' hurt your gunhand.' Ricketts had a deep, growly voice and the smile, such as it was, didn't reflect in his very blue eyes.

'I've got another.'

The smile faded. 'Smart mouth, huh? That don't go down too well at Chain, mister.'

'I'll try and remember.' Brett nodded as he gripped with the other two cowboys, run-of-the-mill ranch hands, both in their mid-twenties. The rail-lean one was Chow — must be his slitty eyes that earned him the name, Brett thought — and the other, a little heavier and sporting a droopy moustache called himself McCracken.

'Just Mack'll do.'

'Seems about right.' Brett grinned and Mack grinned back.

'Get the buckboard loaded,' Lindeen told them, flicked his gaze to Ricketts. 'Thought you'd've had it done already, Harve.'

'We just got here. Seen the stage dust comin' in and decided to wait at the depot.' There was no hint of apology in the big ramrod's tone: just stating the facts.

'What took you so long getting in? I sent my wire a day and a half ago.'

'Them damn mustangs. Started to quit the canyon. I had a few of the boys tip down a couple boulders at one end and throw up a brush fence at the other.' Ricketts glanced at Brett. 'Figured to save our new wrangler some time — and work. An' he sure looks like he should be grateful.'

'Guess I am,' Brett told him. 'Long as those boulders didn't cripple any of the broncs.'

Ricketts's eyes narrowed. 'You think I'm a greenhorn? Goddamn, feller, I know ranch work, was born to it! You'd be wise to 'member that . . . and that I'm the ramrod here.'

Brett nodded. That was all. Lindeen frowned a little. 'Ease up, Harve. Brett's entitled to ask questions.'

'Best if he asks 'em so they don't ruffle.' Ricketts turned his horse abruptly, snapped at Mack in the buckboard seat: 'Get on down to Fiddler's and load up. Lend a hand, Chow. Then head on back to Chain. Mr Lindeen's in a hurry.'

He's pushing it! Brett thought. Wonder if it's usual — or just for my benefit? Showing how tough he thinks he is . . .

'And *you* go on ahead, Harve,' Lindeen said and Brett knew Ricketts had slightly overstepped the line. 'Brett and I'll follow. What made you bring my palomino?'

'Figured you'd want to see him right away. He is your favourite, ain't he?'

'He is. But I prefer to use him on Chain, not these potholed trails. Best keep your mind on your work, Harve. By the by, Brett's answerable only to me until we knock those mustangs into shape. Till then, give him three or four good men. He'll tell you what he wants done.'

Ricketts frowned, sliding his gaze towards Brett. 'Din' know he was that good.'

'We'll all find out.'

Ricketts smothered an epithet, yanked his horse's head around sharply so that Brett had to dodge, then used his spurs to set it off along the winding trail out of town.

'Good foreman?'

Lindeen smiled faintly at Brett's casual question. 'Good as you'll find round here or anywhere else in the territory, I suspect.' He paused. 'Harve's a hard man, very hard, but he gets the job done — and well. So I have to give him a little leeway.'

Brett mounted his sorrel stiffly, immediately feeling the tightening of the horse's skin as its muscles bunched. It snorted, shook its head as he put tension on the reins. It hadn't long been broke to the saddle! Ricketts likely chose it specially for him. Subtle!

Brett clenched with his knees, eased the reins slightly until the horse turned its head, then tightened them sharply, pulling the head all the way round. Before the startled animal could protest, he ran a hand down the long slope to the muzzle, patted it confidently and spoke gently into the big ear. Brown eyes rolled towards him. Muscles bunched more tightly. Then, as he continued to talk in that quiet, easy voice, they slowly relaxed. He gently tweaked the ear with the pale tip as he leaned down, ran his hand over the neck as far as he could reach, talking all the while.

It took several minutes and then the horse snorted a couple of times, moved in a jerky circle. It looked to Lindeen as though it was about to lunge away in a run that would take it clear to the border before it stopped.

But suddenly the animal was still, standing in a more relaxed, though still suspicious, attitude.

'Harve'll be disappointed.'

Brett winked. 'We're not there yet.'

* * *

It took two more weeks to get the horses into shape.

Brett was still too tender in the ribs to do any of the bronc-busting himself but he gave the benefit of his long experience to a promising young cowboy named Chuck Iles. Brett saw right away that the boy had a natural affinity with animals; he fed woodchucks and squirrels of an evening after supper. He was particularly good with horses and even the wild ones, who would bite a chunk out of the corral rails or kick a hole in the barn door, ate apples out of his hand with a gentleness that surprised Brett — and he had seen a lot of wild horses over the years.

He had some of the less seasoned hands work the rough stuff, roping from the mob, dragging the chosen animal to the nubbing post where a flailing sack got it slowly used to movements close up, fighting all the way. There were some unavoidable bites and a lot of cussing as hot tar was applied to the area. A couple of keen hands, wanting to show off, waited in the wings, barely able to contain themselves, figuring they could out-smart any damn animal and ride it to a standstill.

Brett saw that they got plenty of chances to try. Once they hit the saddle, the bone-jarring buck-jumping and stomach-twisting sunfishing started instantly. They never did learn how to fly properly, coming in time and time again for bruising, hide-scraping landings. Luckily, they were able to limp away, with torn shirts hanging from waistbands, muttering, 'To hell with the lousy jughead!' or words to that effect.

But there were some who put an effort in and by the fourth day Brett had three smaller breaking corrals built, with a rider and bucking, stomping horse working in each.

Ricketts came and stood beside him as he watched one older cowhand moving his body expertly with the wild-eyed horse between his legs, rolling easily, one arm flailing, the other hand twisted in the short reins.

'I been waitin' to see you in the saddle.'

Brett didn't take his eyes off the rider. 'You'll see me on the trail.'

The ramrod snorted contemptuously. 'After someone else has done the rough stuff for you!'

'Still looking for volunteers, Harve. You up for it?'

Harve Ricketts spat. 'Got more sense than to risk breakin' my neck on a hoss someone else has busted.'

'I arranged with Lindeen for those boys to get extra pay. That's why there's so many of 'em volunteering.'

Ricketts's big jaw thrust out even further. 'No one told me that!'

'I could fix it for you, too, if you volunteer.'

'Seems to me you've fixed a lot of things with Lindeen I dunno about.'

'Well, I guess he'd tell you if he wanted you to know, Harve.'

Ricketts pushed off the rail he had been leaning on, fists knotted. 'By God, you damn well are a smart-mouth, ain't you!'

'Relax, Harve. I'm not bucking for your job.'

That was it. Ricketts swung and Brett was knocked back several feet before he cannoned off a corner post and fell awkwardly. Someone yelled 'Fight!' and Harve grinned as he stalked in, boots swinging: no concessions for Brett, still recovering from his beating. But Brett managed to twist aside from Harve's boot, though even that hurt his still bruised ribcage. Harve ended kicking the corner post and he cursed, danced about grabbing at his throbbing foot.

Brett got his feet under him, stepped up and slammed two rapid-fire blows into Ricketts's back. The foreman gasped and fell to his knees, startled, blinking. Brett lifted a knee into his face and stretched out the big man in the dust. Harve's head slid under the rail, into the work area.

The rider in the corral had lost his concentration, standing in the stirrups so as to get a better view of the brawl he and others hoped was brewing. The horse sensed this and suddenly the startled rider sailed out of leather as the horse gave way to a series of snorting, back-arched, stiff-legged stomps, crashing into the corral rails and scattering a few cowboys who had been clambering up to watch. Ricketts's eyes widened and he struggled to get his head and big shoulders back under the low rail as the hoofs thudded down, spattering his contorted face with clods of dirt. Hot spittle from the horse's mouth splattered against his face and he yelled as the hoofs rose above him with murderous intent.

Then someone grabbed his legs and he was yanked out from under, unceremoniously, face scraping against the bottom rail, the back of his head dragging through the dirt. He heard the hoofs slam down, felt the jar through the earth as he was rolled away to safety. The horse slammed into the rails and he was sure he heard the timber splinter.

He was startled to see Brett standing over him, offering a dirt-caked hand to help him up. Dazed, bleeding, Ricketts stood, swaying. Brett steadied him.

'Why'd it have to be you!'

'That's all right, Harve. You're welcome.'

Ricketts stared long and hard at his rescuer. 'I'd've left you.'

Brett smiled. 'I somehow figured that.'

Harve frowned, wiping a kerchief around his face with a hand that shook a little. 'But you still dragged me out . . . ?'

Brett shrugged and turned away. The cowboys who had gathered looked disappointed that there wasn't going to be a knock-down, drag-out fight, after all. They all knew Brett would have lost, anyway, with his ribs still taped, limping on bruised legs, one eye still swollen and half shut, purple-green like a summer-storm sky.

Rickett's big hand fell on the mustanger's shoulder. Brett turned warily, but as fast as his aching bones would allow. Harve scratched at the dirt-clogged stubble on his jaw. 'S'pose I oughta thank you.'

'Only if you feel the need, Harve. Doesn't worry me.'

Ricketts looked relieved, smiled crookedly as he dropped the hand he had started to proffer. 'That's OK then.' He rounded on the gaping cowhands. 'All right! What the hell you starin' at? Show's over. Git back to work. Date limit's approachin' an' Mr Lindeen's a stickler for keepin' to his schedule.'

The men scattered and Ricketts took his crushed hat from Chuck Iles, punched it roughly into shape and jammed it on his head as he turned away.

'Think I mighta let him lie,' the kid said and Brett shook his head.

'You wouldn't've.'

'Nah — s'pose not. Woulda thought about it, though.'

★   ★   ★

It was time for the last of the support bandages and pads to come off. Brett couldn't get rid of them fast enough.

He had followed the doctor's instructions and kept them on for the prescribed time but he was itchy and knew he must smell like a polecat, for he hadn't been able to take a bath or even have a proper wash in case he wet the padding.

Now, riding his sorrel towards the creek at the extreme edge of Chain's north line, he decided this was as far as he was prepared to go. He dismounted and tied the reins securely to a low willow branch; the horse was not yet fully trusting and might easily decide to wander off. Under the willow's drooping foliage, he stripped buck naked.

It was a good day for plunging into cool creek water out of the sun. He enjoyed splashing around, swam a few strokes but as soon as he felt pain starting in his torso he stopped and waded back into the shallows. Here he sat down and with handfuls of sand from the creekbed he scrubbed away the scaling flesh that had been covered by the support padding for so long.

It sure felt good. He did a little patch at a time, and reached as far around his back as he could. Then simply sat there, luxuriating . . .

He had ridden around Hondo Basin, not only to get the lie of the land, but also to meet the other ranchers who were adding their cattle to the combined drive. Most of them were happy to include their few cows with Lindeen's; they would get a better price at the Bensonville market than they could locally. But one or two seemed a mite apprehensive although they wouldn't put their anxiety into words.

'Let's just say, I'm short of cash so I'm gonna take the chance,' one family man told him, Whit Bingham.

'What chance? With only a hundred or so head, it's a small percentage of the big herd. Lindeen calculates on five to seven thousand — that's why he's asked each rancher to send along at least one rider. Your lot'll be safe enough.'

'I know that and I should go myself. My son's too young and my wife don't want me to leave her here. So Lindeen says that's OK, long as I realize there'll be a deduction from the sale price for one of his crew handlin' my cows on the drive.'

Brett hadn't known that, but he ran up against it with a couple of other ranchers, too.

No wonder Lindeen was the richest man in Hondo Basin, if not this part of New Mexico Territory.

This was a glimpse of the man's harder side — the business side. No sentiment, just hard, cold cash.

But others were willing, either to supply riders or pay the 'driving fee' as Lindeen termed it. It was fair enough though someone as rich as Lindeen could have waived it.

The flats where the herd was being held were a virtual sea of cattle now, stretching almost to the edge of the line of sawtooth hills to the north-west.

They would stretch for miles out along what was to become known as the Rio Hondo Trail.

Out of the corner of his eye Brett suddenly saw movement as someone ducked in under the willow. He turned quickly, ignoring the stab of pain it cost him, and slid his Colt out of the holster which he left resting with his cartridge belt on a flat rock within easy reach, but high and dry.

The intruder was a young girl, dressed in work-soiled denim trousers, the cuffs tucked into the tops of worn half-boots. She wore a checked shirt with a calfskin vest over it, and a curl-brim hat sat on the back of a head of dark-brown hair that hung to just above her shoulders.

Her face was round, although she wasn't plump in the body, and her lips were full and red, but drawing out into a thinner line even as he watched. Hazel eyes narrowed.

'Do you always bathe with a gun?'

'Only when I'm not expecting a

handsome young lady.'

'Don't try sweet-talking me. You're Lindeen's gunfighter, aren't you?'

'I'm Calvin Brett and I work for Charles Lindeen.'

'As his gunfighter!' she insisted. 'We've heard all about you, Brett.'

'Then how about joining me? We could toss a heap of pointless gossip back and forth while you scrub my back . . . '

He was surprised to see her face redden — but not with anger. She was embarrassed. 'How dare you!'

'Hey, it wasn't meant as an insult. In fact, it wasn't meant any way at all, just something that jumped into my head.'

'Well, I'm not about to jump into the creek — with you or any other man, 'specially not one of Lindeen's!'

'What's wrong with Charley? I've found him all right.' He was genuinely interested for he had picked up on several occasions during his ride round the basin that Lindeen wasn't too popular. But envy for the rich and powerful was nothing new and he had figured that was all it was. But this girl somehow put a different slant on things. Her dislike was much stronger.

She leaned against the tree, toying with fronds of the branches, studying him. 'You sound genuinely . . . perplexed. Either that, or you go along with his arrogance and roughshod tactics — which, of course, you would, wouldn't you, Brett! Being on his payroll as a hired gun.'

'Lady, you got the better of me as far as names go.'

'I'm Meg Hatch.' She waved a hand languidly in a general south-west direction. 'I run Lazy H with my father.'

Brett nodded. 'Yeah, think I spoke with him earlier. He's putting in a couple of hundred head with the big herd, isn't he?' She nodded, lips tight. 'Sending a rider, too . . . ' He added this slowly, a hunch scratching at him. 'Not . . . you by any chance?'

She pushed off the tree, straightening

to her full height of about five feet six inches. 'I suppose you're going to tell me, too, that a trail drive is no place for a woman!'

'Well, it's not, but if you already know that and still aim to go, it's no use me saying any more about it.'

She seemed taken aback at the answer, frowned, and waited a few moments before speaking again. 'Yes, I do intend to ride along — keep an eye on our herd and make sure we aren't cheated out of what's rightfully ours.'

'That's a bit hard, isn't it? Lindeen seems honest enough to me.'

'Oh? You think so? Why don't you ask some of the smaller spreads who *aren't* sending their cattle with the big herd? Ask them how they've been crowded into one corner of the basin, all the small spreads together — hardly room to run a few cows on the miserable pieces of dirt Lindeen's left for them! Their crops grow well enough but there's more money in cattle than vegetables.'

'Meg, they're *nesters*, not ranchers,' he said with the cattleman's inbred dislike of farmers utilizing good grazing land. 'I talked with one man, Rupe someone — '

'Rupe Middleton. He started out with fifty mixed head of cattle, milkers and beef, but ended up selling them all to Lindeen for a pittance — in exchange for being allowed to keep his spread.'

'*Allowed* to keep his spread? Does Lindeen own the land?'

'Almost the entire basin south of the creek. You haven't done your homework very well, it seems, Brett!' She sounded quite pleased at having found that out.

'I take folk as I find 'em, Meg'

'I'm Miss Hatch to you!'

'OK, *Miss* Hatch. I found Lindeen to my liking. He's a rich man and I guess all rich men have their faults, as seen by poorer men, but I'm happy to be working for him.'

'Then you're probably as miserable a human being as he is!' She turned abruptly, saw his piled clothing and paused to kick it all over the river bank, leaving one sleeve of the shirt actually trailing in the water.

He burst out laughing, couldn't help himself.

'That's the best first-grade tantrum I've seen a full-grown woman throw in a coon's age!' He raised his voice as she angrily clawed a way out of the drooping fronds. 'I'll look for you on the trail drive!'

Her voice was sharp and he knew she was determined to have the last word. 'Maybe you'd better! I'm a damn fine shot with a rifle!'

He was still chuckling to himself when he stood up, letting the water run from his lean, scarred body, hearing her horse racing away at full gallop.

But after he was dressed and had stepped out from under the willow, his chuckle faded. Abruptly.

She was riding a white horse with a smattering of grey dots on its rump — *and leading his sorrel!*

'Damn the woman! girl — whatever she is! She'll probably be miles away before she decides to turn it loose! And a damn fat lot of good that'll do me!'

He swore bitterly as he felt the hammering heat of the noon sun. Then, resigned, he jammed on his hat, buckled his gunbelt around his waist and started walking.

It was going to be a long, long, hot afternoon.

6

Jailbreak

He was known as 'Dutchy'. He had another name and some men knew it but no one bothered to call him anything but 'Dutchy', unless it was 'that squarehead son of a bitch' or something equally descriptive along those lines.

He arrived in the territorial prison on the early morning wagon and his face was still cut and scraped, bleeding a little, where the careless barber had removed his Vandyck beard. Strangely, that had subdued Dutchy who, up till that time, had been loud and relentless in his complaining about the food and lack of regular washing facilities and a host of other things that didn't suit him.

But when he was ordered to have his

beard removed — 'all facial hair', said the regulations and that included moustaches and sideburns — and his hair cropped, Dutchy seemed to lose a lot of confidence. *Something* left him, along with the soapy clumps of hair that fell into his lap.

So he sulked and kept to himself in the wagon, once viciously jabbing a thumb into the eye of another prisoner who riled him one time too many. Then he was left alone.

When he arrived with the others at the prison compound he sought a place in the shade of one high stone wall, sat down with his back against it, arms on his knees, hands dangling. Judging by his facial expression, whatever he was thinking about brought him little joy. Then a shadow fell across him and Dutchy looked up slowly, ready for trouble.

'Hardly knew you at first, Dutchy. That barber's a goddamn Genghis Khan once he gets that blunt razor in his fist, ain't he?'

Dutchy squinted, moved his head a little so the sun wasn't blinding him. Then he started to scramble to his feet.

'Ripley! Judas, man, I thought they hung you.'

Tad Ripley leaned on the wall, laughed, showing his bared, gritted teeth in what for him passed as a smile — his trademark.

'They tried, but here I am. Goddamn sheriff named Bolan *wanted* the hangin' scrapped, 'cause I'd wounded him in the shoot-out, nicked his lung, and he had to retire from badge-totin'. 'Give the bastard life, Judge!' he said. 'Give him years to think about what a damn fool he's been — an' let him swing that sledge till the day he dies!'' Ripley spat. 'You b'lieve it? Damn judge went along with him and me and Yank and Boots got life on the rockpile! If that lousy McCabe weren't already dead I'd dig my way out with a spoon an' go strangle the bastard. Was him got Bolan so damned riled up.'

Dutchy looked at him squarely. 'Brett ain't dead.'

Ripley stiffened, just as Yank Bilby and Boots Skene sauntered up, nodding to Dutchy.

'The hell you say! Bolan told me he died out in the badlands. They found his hoss where he'd shot it. No saddle-bags, though.' Ripley frowned. 'He had the money from the Telford Express with him, you know. Ambush hit us an' wasn't time to spread it around between us. He had the lot!'

'Dunno about that, but I was workin' with Buckskin. You 'member Buckskin Rance? Yeah, thought you would. Well, we seen Brett McCabe win a good stake up at Ryker's Outpost an' he had all the signs of a man about to jump a boxcar. So Buckskin set it up and we rolled him.'

Ripley was leaning forward now, mouth tight, face pinched with interest. 'And . . . ?'

'Well. Kind of embarrassin', Tad — '
'Get on with it!'

'He threw me off the damn train! I was mighty poorly when I came round. Train long gone, of course, Buckskin, too. I got picked up by a deputy who took me to Bensonville.'

'Hell, that's Casmeier's bailiwick, ain't it?' said Yank Bilby in his thin voice. 'Stay away from him!'

Dutchy nodded, a brief flare in his eyes as he remembered. 'Anyways, Casmeier tossed me in jail an' damn me if McCabe don't come to the cell bars and identify me as one of the fellers who jumped him.' He shook his head slowly. 'Casmeier dug up a dodger on me from that time I was ridin' with Bloody Pete Magill an' here I am. Twenty years to look forward to in this shit-hole.'

'You'll be out before us,' grunted Boots Skene. 'We got life.'

Tad Ripley gave him a sidelong glance, his rugged face looking very sober. 'Don't mean we'll be here all that time.'

Yank and Boots raised their eyebrows

and Dutchy frowned. 'I heard this place is impossible to bust out of.'

'That's what they say. But I figure anyone with enough incentive could find some way out.'

Yank Bilby pursed his lips. 'Them wall guards shoot to kill, Tad. Just one thing goes wrong, they'll nail you.'

Ripley scowled. 'Gimme a choice between pulverizin' rocks into a handful of gravel and riskin' a bullet while tryin' to escape an' I know damn well which I'll take.'

That corner of the compound was silent for what seemed to drag on for minutes. Then Boots ventured, 'What's this . . . incentive, Tad, that's strong enough for you to even think about such foolishness?'

Skene stepped back hurriedly as Ripley turned towards him.

'McCabe's still alive!'

'Hell, you can't be sure — '

'Listen, I seen him! He was breathin' right in my face before he threw me off that train! It was him, all right.' Dutchy was indignant and there was an edge of anger in his voice as he glared at Boots for doubting him.

'Well, if he was playin' poker with Ryker's tinhorns an' ridin' the rails, it sure don't look to me like he still has the bank money,' Boots pointed out.

'He'd've stashed it,' Ripley said. 'Goddamn, he was the last man ridin' out of that ambush Bolan laid for us in Telford — the *last man!* Yet he was the one got clean away — an' carryin' the loot!' His eyes seemed to flare as they settled on Boots Skene. 'That enough reason for you?'

Skene looked uncertain. 'Would be pretty to think we might pick up that cash again, Tad, but . . . ' He waved his long, bony hands around at the crowded compound, and the armed guards patrolling the walls.

'There's some way outta here besides in a pine box — an' I aim to find it!' Ripley glared at the others again, showing that taut, meaningless smile. 'Them that wants to come is welcome.

The more the merrier.'

Dutchy returned Tad's look soberly. 'More targets for the damn guards!'

Ripley's smile only widened. 'And that's a bad thing?'

★ ★ ★

Most of Stallion Forks turned out to watch the biggest trail herd ever seen in that part of the country leave for the distant meat market in the north.

There were gathered together almost forty riders, three chuckwagons, another three buckboards weighed down with all kinds of spare gear and wet-weather clothing, medical supplies and emergency hardtack; four more wagons packed tight with bales of hay in case there were more patches with feed thin on the ground than Lindeen's scouts had found; a blacksmith's wagon with a portable forge and a heavy load of bar iron and extra horsehoes; together 6,500 shuffling, lowing steers. There was a dust cloud that stretched for miles over the

Hondo Basin, even dulling the rays of the early-morning sun.

Folk cheered, threw hats into the air and kids ran about earning mild curses from the riders. Lindeen's sale of this herd would bring a slew of money into Stallion Forks, one way and another. More work, too, as it was rumoured that he aimed to extend Chain, throw up more line shacks and barns, fence in more land.

Of course, not everyone was pleased at that prospect, but most folk realized that the Hondo Basin was on its way to becoming a mighty important part of this territory's future. The wild element was gradually leaving the basin and families were settling in. Some clashed with Lindeen's ambitions but one way or another it was eventually sorted out. He was a tough man, but as fair as he could make it.

Not always to the satisfaction of the nesters or quarter-section hopefuls, but *almost* always to Lindeen's. Day by day, Brett McCabe had seen how hard the man could be when business was involved. Nothing much was ever going to stand in the way of Lindeen achieving his aims, that was certain. He was tight-fisted at times, but whoever he dealt with always left or capitulated with *something* in their pockets.

Twice Brett had seen Lindeen, on the quiet, send a couple of his ranch hands to help out someone he had been 'negotiating' with. Womenfolk, despite their bitter disappointment at times, had nothing but praise for his gentlemanly manner and his kindness to children. Of course, buying a bag of cherry strap-candy was nothing to Lindeen, but it made the right impression.

Most folk agreed he was a hard man, but if anyone was going to put the Hondo Basin on the map, it was Charley Lindeen.

Meg Hatch was riding along, as promised, and her father had tagged on, too, no doubt worried about her being the lone woman amongst all these hard-living men. Yet, whatever lascivious thoughts they might have had were kept amongst themselves and any man stupid enough to try and force his attentions on Meg would have found himself dancing the Rio two-step from the nearest cottonwood at the end of a rope.

That was, if she didn't shoot him first.

Milo Hatch was smarter than he looked, thought Brett. He had his daughter put on an impromptu demonstration, setting things up to show her prowess with a rifle, under the pretext of shooting it in after damaging the sights when she had dropped the weapon over a rock ledge. *Maybe* . . .

She not only destroyed a row of beer bottles at fifty yards within seconds, but then proceeded to shatter the remaining few inches of the necks, which were still swinging from the cords that held them to the low-slung branch of a tree. The cook had then been induced to hand over his small, flat essence bottles, after decanting the contents into other, larger containers. (He drank some, '*Just to empty the dregs*.') The original bottles, only three or four inches high, and slim — not quite half an inch thick — were placed edge-on in a line on a log.

She didn't miss a single one and Brett smiled to himself as he watched the faces of the cowboys who had come to jeer, but stayed to cheer. There were a lot of disappointed, low-slung jaws and regretful eyes; he knew Meg was entirely safe now.

No man would be loco enough to lay a hand on her or make an off-colour suggestion to her after that shooting demonstration. Especially as Milo Hatch said casually, 'Guess I taught her pretty good.'

Lindeen grinned at Brett. 'There go a few fantasies.'

'About thirty-six, I reckon.'

'Maybe thirty-seven?' Lindeen suggested, giving Brett the suggestion of a leer.

Brett shook his head, smiling. 'Uh-uh. I met her down at the creek and she took my sorrel and left me with a seven-mile hike in the sun, remember?'

'She's feisty,' Lindeen agreed. Suddenly he called '*Hey!*' He wheeled his palomino and ran it fast around the outskirts of the herd, down towards the drag.

'Clete! Mungo! Watch those calves, damn it! They've separated from the mothers and they'll get trampled . . . '

Eagle-eyed even when he was joshing or having a light conversation, Brett thought. Not much escaped Charles Lindeen's notice.

He made a bet with himself, that the losses on this trail drive would be the lowest anyone had ever recorded.

Then he turned his sorrel and cut across to nudge back some of his *remuda* that showed signs of wanting to wander towards the bright-green grass showing on a nearby hogback.

This was going to be one long, mighty busy trail drive.

And each step took him further away from a town called Telford.

★ ★ ★

The prison warden was a short, hard-eyed man with receding wavy hair and impressive mutton chops. His button nose and lopsided mouth did nothing to make him look any more prepossessing. Nothing could, right at this moment, as he stared bleakly at the two prisoners standing before him, ankle chains and wrist manacles in place, their grimy, torn clothes stinking of sweat, old food and dried mud.

'See these two are hosed down when I've finished with 'em. And you might change your own uniforms,' he barked.

The guards looked little better than the prisoners, hulking, bully-boys, endlessly fingering their hardwood billies, just waiting for a word or a sign from the warden so they could crack a prisoner's skull or slam him behind the knees, bringing him down, sobbing in pain.

'You're a bigger fool than I allowed, Ripley,' the warden grated suddenly, leaning back in his chair. 'You've been here long enough to know you can't possibly escape, yet you and this fool you call Boots — where, I suspect what few brains he has, reside — made a try even the village idiot would've rejected.'

'Warden, what do we have to lose?' asked Ripley, sucking on a newly split lip, wanting to hawk blood running down behind his battered nose but making himself hold back — for now.

The warden's thin lips moved and there was a kind of neighing sound. Then Ripley and Boots realized the warden was laughing.

'Lose? Hell, haven't you worked it out yet? You think I'll end your daily suffering by having you hung for trying to escape? Put an end to all the hell that's still awaiting you? Chris'sakes, man, you are a damn halfwit!' He glanced at the grey-faced Boots whose nose, hammered to one side of his face, was dripping blood. 'I won't even bother talking to this dummy; he'd follow you to hell because he knows no better. But how did you ever think you

102

stood a chance of getting away with making a sling and knocking out a wall guard with a rock from it?'

'It was a good shot, Warden, you gotta gimme that.' Ripley showed his trademark smile, watching the warden blink in astonishment: *a prisoner talking back to him, in a frivolous manner, in his own office, too! Had Ripley gone loco . . . ?*

'By God, I do believe all those hours in the sun on the rockpile have addled what little brains you've got, Ripley!' He nodded to the biggest guard, a young brute called Smasher by the prison population. 'Show him the error of his ways.'

Smasher moved in, heavy features expressionless, the billy driving upwards towards Ripley's solar plexus. It landed and Ripley staggered back a couple of paces, but he didn't go down or double over, though he coughed loudly. And what was that dull clunk . . . ?

There was a double square of sheet iron, the edges rolled, lined with rags and tied across Ripley's mid-section with rawhide strips under his shirt — like armour plate, protecting his midriff, the guards' favourite target.

But the warden's biggest surprise came when Ripley's manacled hands fumbled at the loose folds of his torn and sagging clothing, came out with an open clasp knife. The blade slashed across Smasher's throat as he stepped in. The man stopped dead, gurgled and clapped both hands to his severed carotid artery. Blood sprayed across the desk and on to the warden and the wall. As Smasher dropped to his knees and his companion guard stood, thunderstruck, jaw dropping as he stared, Boots drew a knife, too, made from a piece of file laboriously shaped and honed on the stone cell floor over many long, tense nights.

He buried it to the rag-wrapped hilt in the second guard's chest. By that time, Ripley was beside the warden's chair, holding his dripping knife blade to the man's throat.

'Sure, Warden, a real stupid move slingin' a rock at the wall guard. But it got us brought here and the guards were havin' so much fun kickin' our asses they didn't even search us. An' you won't even get a chance to roast their nuts.'

He pressed the knife blade and the warden made a whimpering sound as blood oozed from the shallow cut.

'You're right, Warden. There's no way anyone can *bust* outa this hell-hole. The walls and floors and doors are all too thick or heavy. Waste of strength tryin'. Too many guards, all told to shoot to kill. But there's a weakness in your system.' He thrust his battered face close to the warden's. 'Yourself, and thesc bastards you hire as guards!'

He kicked Smasher who was close to death now, marble white and sunken-looking, his blood flooding across the floor beneath the warden's desk, eyes dull as stones.

Ripley yanked the shaking warden to his feet, slammed him violently into the wall. 'Get your key and unlock our chains, Warder. Then send for Yank Bilby and Dutchy. We're all goin' outa here in one happy party with you in the lead. Unless you try somethin' real stupid, then none of us is goin' anywhere but to hell. But you'll be first.'

Unable to contain himself any longer, he beat the warden to the floor with his fists and the iron manacles. Boots joined him in kicking the man until Ripley regained control, pushed Boots back. Both men were panting.

'Better not stomp him too much,' Ripley panted. 'We need him for a while yet.'

The bloodstained, semi-conscious warden cowered behind his hands as Ripley grinned down at him.

'Just for a *leetle* while!' He shook his head sadly. 'I just don't see you got much of a future, Warden. Not much at all! An' *by Christ!* that makes me happy! Only thing that'll make me happier is when I catch up with that double-crossin' Brett McCabe.'

7

North to Danger

Hardly a man on the whole trail crew rode without a bandanna tied over the lower half of his face.

The pall of dust raised by the slogging, bawling cantankerous herd could be seen for miles and spread over many acres of country as the herd was driven slowly north, nudged along by the hot winds. Riding drag was hell. Grit was in everything, in every bodily orifice and crease of clothing. Eating was accompanied by an irritating *crunch-crunch!* as grit was mashed with the food between the teeth. If a man cleared his nose, he blew mud. If he spat, it was the same thing. Eyes were permanently reddened and mattery, some riders having to quit for a day or two as their eyelids swelled up. The only treatment was to bathe the eyes with water boiled by the cook and allowed to cool.

No one would drink the stream or well water they infrequently found, until it had been boiled by the cook. It was an order given and strictly enforced by Charles Lindeen.

'There're enough reasons why a man can pick up a bellyache without even trying. No sense in making it easy by drinking dirty water.'

He fired two men who found it too inconvenient to wash their hands thoroughly with soap and water before eating. One rode off happily enough but the other, Beanpole, had to air his complaints.

'Damned old woman!' he bitched. 'Christ, I grew up with five sisters and my mom. I never had this kinda stuff. We had no more bellyaches than anyone else as I recall.'

'That's why you're so damn skinny now,' Harve Ricketts told him roughly. 'Need two of you to even throw a shadow. Now pack your gear an' light out.'

The man still grumbled, so Harve hauled off and swung a big fist into the narrow face. The cowhand dropped on the spot, knocked cold. Harve automatically drew back his boot but Lindeen, bringing Beanpole's pay, stopped him dead.

'Quit that, Harve! The man's got enough trouble being fired way out here, miles from any town and likely a hundred miles from his home.'

'A hard lesson won't do no one any harm, Mr Lindeen,' Ricketts said, surly, indicating the other hands at their various jobs. 'Beat on one man, show him the errors of his ways, you mayn't have to fire another one.'

Lindeen held Harve's angry gaze, pushed some bills and a few coins into his calloused hand. 'Give this to Beanpole when he comes round — and let him have his pick of the *remuda* for a horse to get him back to civilization.'

'The *pick*! Judas, there're some fine-lookin' hosses there, boss! He ain't worth that.'

'Do it, Harve, and then keep the men

moving. We can push through to Jagged Creek by sundown or a little later. Everyone'll rest easier near good water, including the herd.'

Lindeen mounted and rode off. Harve watched, still surly, and when the cattleman rode slowly down into a hollow Harve turned to Beanpole.

He was just starting to come round. Groggily, he sat up. Ricketts strode across and rammed the man's pay into his torn shirt pocket. He backhanded him across the face, steadied to keep him from falling.

'Find that sway-backed jughead you rode in here an' git. You're still around in an hour, I'll tear your head off.'

The man looked fearful, running a tongue around the inside of his newly split lips. He scrambled awkwardly to his feet. Harve scowled again and turned to his own horse. He stopped dead when he saw Brett sitting his sorrel a few yards away, watching him.

'You want somethin'?' the foreman growled.

'Just passed Mr Lindeen. He said to make sure Beanpole had a horse good enough to see him to the next town.'

'He's got his own mount.'

'The boss must think it's not good enough.'

Harve walked over and stood beside the sorrel, hands on hips, as he looked up at Brett. '*I* think it's good enough.'

'Tell Lindeen, then. Problem's all yours now.' Brett started to pull the sorrel's head around, but Harve swore, grabbed Brett's leg and heaved. The big horse swung away with a whicker and Brett grabbed at the mane to keep himself from falling. Harve heaved again and Brett tumbled to the ground, rolling quickly away from the horse's hoofs.

Riders who were working the edges of the herd close by rode across as they saw what was happening. Harve was already standing with boots planted solidly, big fists knotted.

'S'pose you'll claim sore ribs again?' he sneered.

Dusting himself down with his hat,

Brett said, 'They're still plenty sore, all right.'

Harve scoffed and spat. 'Knew you was yeller.' He started to turn away, throwing an 'I told you so' glance at the riders coming in. There was a swagger to him now and he stumbled as Brett grabbed one beefy shoulder and pulled him off balance, twisting him around.

Harve hardly had time to see Brett remove his old hat when the stiff, dusty felt slammed across his face. It *hurt* and Ricketts stumbled, one hand going to his nose, already feeling warm blood trickling from his nostrils. He straightened, his mouth bloody now, and, with a roar, he charged back. Brett stepped aside and hit him hard again across one ear with the hat. He swung it backhanded, left-right, half a dozen times, fast and hard, each time getting Harve full in the face. He was off balance and staggering, went down to one knee. Brett stepped in, lifted a knee under Rickett's jaw and its impact flung the big ramrod on to his back.

Shaking his head, blood streaking

across his reddened, swelling cheeks, Harve rolled and came up, throwing a handful of dirt at Brett's head. Brett dodged and Harve was waiting, driving a fist into the side of the other's neck. Brett went down on one knee and expecting a boot or a driving knee from Ricketts, threw himself sideways. Harve missed with his kick, stumbled.

Brett came up behind him, sledged a fist on to Harve's spine, grabbed his belt at the back and a handful of the thick, fair hair. Ricketts yelled, hands going up, trying to break the grip: his hair felt as though it was being pulled out by the roots — and it was. But only long enough for Brett to give a mighty heave that sent the ramrod into the small campfire where someone was drying a pair of boots.

Harve yelled and, in momentary panic, began to beat at his smouldering clothes. Brett kicked the legs out from under him. This time when Ricketts rolled on to his back he snatched at his Colt.

Harve froze the movement with a sharp and clearly audible indrawing of breath. Brett's Colt was already in his fist, hammer cocked, and Harve knew death was staring him in the face. Scarcely daring to breathe now, he released his hold on his gun butt and lifted his hands out from his sides.

'You could be dead right now, Harve,' Brett told him, putting away the gun and punching his hat into some kind of shape before putting it on his head. As he straightened it, he saw Meg Hatch amongst the riders who had stopped work to watch.

She was sitting her white horse with the dappling of grey, her face blank as she looked down at him.

Brett touched a hand to the crumpled brim of his hat, nodding slightly. Without change of expression she turned the horse and rode on back to her position beside the herd as it plodded slowly by.

Lindeen walked his palomino in from the lip of the hollow. His gaze sought Brett. 'I'm glad you had sense enough not to use that gun. A stampede is the last thing we need.'

'Just looking at it was enough for Harve. Knew I wouldn't have to shoot.'

Ricketts scowled and swore. 'You're a lousy fighter, Brett.'

'I'm not the one bleeding,' Brett pointed out. Harve started forward, fists clenching.

'All right, that's enough!' Lindeen set the palomino between the men. 'I need both of you or you'd be drawing your time right now. Any more of this and I'll kick you out, regardless. Understood?'

Brett nodded but Harve took a minute to use a kerchief on his bleeding mouth and nose before he looked over the blood-spattered cloth and jerked a nod at Lindeen.

'Now get back to your positions — all of you!'

The riders scattered. Brett remounted stiffly and rode towards the *remuda* he had left in charge of Chuck Iles.

Harve took time to berate two or three cowboys before going to his own horse and swinging into saddle. He rode back to work, still holding the crumpled kerchief against his nose. His ears were purple and starting to swell.

★ ★ ★

The jailbreak had been successful.

It had been what Boots Skene called as easy as shelling peas, taking the warden along with Ripley's knife blade against his spine, Yank Bilby walking close on the other side.

Dutchy trailed a mite nervously with Boots and the warden's wife, a slim, terrified woman in her early fifties. There were family quarters in a secure, fenced-in section of the prison, but the warden had been induced to order the guard on the gate to open up and then go off duty early. As it was sundown by now, there were plenty of shadows to cover the group, and the guard had an assignation in the nearby town, so he needed no further urging.

He was in such a hurry to see his

woman — whose husband worked at the stage depot and this week didn't finish his shift until after nine o'clock — that he never even mentioned the peculiar group accompanying the dazed and sick-looking warden.

It was almost an hour later, at full dark, when Ripley and his men left, with the warden and his wife riding in their buggy, Dutchy driving. By then the prisoners were dressed in guards' clothing and two carried weapons. The men on the gate gave them hardly a second glance as the warden, at Ripley's 'suggestion', berated them for imagined slackness.

Once the gate opened, there was the long, winding trail leading to the town, a pale snake in the starlight.

Freedom.

★   ★   ★

The bodies of the warden and his wife were found late the next day, amidst the buggy's wreckage at the bottom of a gorge upstream from the crossing of the Rio Hondo.

There was no sign of the missing convicts.

A hastily convened posse, a mixture of townsmen and prison guards, searched the countryside frantically for three days without success. By then they concluded the fugitives had crossed the border into Mexico, possibly going by way of El Paso; Ripley was originally from Texas and probably had friends or kinfolk there.

It was the logical place for the fugitives to go and the search around and beyond the Tularosa Valley was now scaled down; Wanted dodgers were printed, a bounty of $2,000 per man offered. No one was sorry that the brutal warden had reached the end of his life, but there was a furore about his wife's murder once details of her obvious suffering before she died were released.

A lot of men searched for the escapees, bounty hunters all. Not one of them thought to search Avalon, the town nearest to the territorial prison; it was figured they would have given such a close place a wide berth.

The quartet had plenty of money now. They had made the warden open his safe and had taken the prison's ready cash with them. It had been one day before the guards' payday and all that cash had been made up in a score or more of slim brown envelopes.

Ripley had timed it well and spread some of that money around to a pair of whores he knew, sisters, who had set up their cabin at the north edge of town.

As a sideline to their most obvious calling they made a small fortune by channelling men on the run down to the border, and so they had a 'waiting' room disguised as a root cellar beneath the roomy cabin.

Ripley, Yank, Boots and Dutchy stayed there for a week, living the life of Riley, well-fed, dressed in good clothes, comforted by the women — at extra cost, naturally — waiting for the fuss to die down. Once word came in that they were reckoned to have reached Mexico, Ripley shelled out $300, almost the last of what they had stolen, and the scraggy blonde called Tess brought them guns, a rifle and a six-gun each, with some boxes of bullets.

When Ripley said that they needed horses and grub for the trail, Tess and her sister, Hester, a busty woman with large teeth, smiled.

'Sure, Tad, me darlin'. It'll be costin' you another two hundred. Horses come cheaper than guns around here but — '

Tess had been doing the talking but it was Hester who gave a small scream of alarm as Ripley lifted the Colt he had just strapped around his waist, after checking it was loaded. He smiled with that tight, gritted-teeth grin.

'Gals, you've been mighty kind, but we've paid our way an' you've bled us white. I b'lieve it's bonus time.' He reached out and grabbed Hester's flabby upper arm, yanking her tightly against him. 'You supply the hosses saddles and grub. We ride away and you never see us again.' The grin tightened. 'You got my word on that.'

And Tad Ripley kept it.

After the mounts were obtained they killed the sisters down in the underground room, then locked it up tight and screened the hidden door. They ransacked the cabin and located the sisters' hoard, found almost $500. Then, in the deep dark of midnight, they quit the cabin after setting it afire. All four were unrecognizable as recently escaped convicts, freshly shaved, hair slicked, wearing decent range clothes which blended in well with those of the men drifting around Avalon.

They aimed to head north-east, skirting the Mescalero Apache reserve and crossing the Rio Hondo, and eventually to slip over the state line into Texas where Ripley hoped to find some of his kinfolk.

But after they crossed the Hondo, with all that money burning holes in their pockets, they couldn't resist the beckoning bright lights of nearby Roswell.

And that was where they met a disgruntled ex-trail-hand working as a saloon swamper. His name was Beanpole.

★ ★ ★

Brett was washing a shirt at the edge of a creek, the herd lowing and snorting and bawling as they settled in for the night's stop on a short-grass plain. They would be restless tonight and tomorrow, too, maybe for longer, until they reached better feed. Good grass had been sparse these last couple of weeks.

Lindeen made a wise move by stopping the drive early, two hours before sundown. The scout had ridden back and reported that the short-grass continued for miles yet, before running into the foothills of a series of ranges that spread out like the fingers on a hand.

No sense in getting any closer to those hills at this time of day: if there happened to be good grass there and the herd caught a whiff of it, they would never settle for the night. This way they were restless but would eventually calm down as the stars appeared and it was evident that they were not going to get anything better.

Brett heard a footstep behind him and instinctively came to his feet, his hand slapping against his gun butt. Big Harve Ricketts smiled crookedly at him.

'That's your real callin', ain't it? Gunslinger, not mustanger.'

'A little of both, Harve.'

Harve leaned a shoulder against a tree, rolling a smoke in the fading light. 'You and me. Just the two of us. No guns. Just fists — see who's the better man.'

'Harve, I care so little about your opinion of me that I just don't care at all.'

Ricketts frowned, stiffening a little. He scratched a match into flame on the bark, cupped a hand and lit up.

'You're scared to find out.'

'Just not interested. Your opinion

means nothing to me, Harve.'

'Listen, you damn *pistolero*! I don't take a beatin' with a hat from no man! I want this settled. But we gotta do it on the quiet or Lindeen'll kick us both off and I like my job.'

Still alert, Brett turned back to rinsing his shirt. 'Then go do it — and quit bothering me.'

Harve grinned. 'I kinda like botherin' you.'

'Keep it up and you'll soon grow tired.'

'Ah, that's better! You gonna punch my head in? Kick my butt?'

Brett sighed. 'I'm gonna ignore you, Harve. Just like I'm trying to do now.'

'Sure! Because you're yeller! Won't fight.'

Brett looked at him over his shoulder, eyes bleak. 'I don't aim to bust my hands on your hard head, Harve. You push this and I'll accommodate you. But I'll beat your head in with a gun barrel.'

Harve stepped away from the tree quickly, alarm flitting across his rugged face. Then he crushed the cigarette out in the palm of his hand without changing expression. His lips tightened and moved as he cussed under his breath. He shook a big forefinger at Brett.

'We got a long ways to go yet to the railhead! You got yours comin'!'

He wheeled and stomped back through the shadowy trees. Brett turned back to his shirt.

Harve Ricketts didn't bother him; he was just a bully, nose out of joint because Lindeen had hired Brett in the first place and gave him a mostly free hand. And because he knew his job and got it done pronto.

He hung the wet shirt on a low branch and when he turned he saw a blur of someone standing in the shadows with a bundle of washing. He had clapped a hand to his gun butt and had the Colt half-drawn before he recognized Meg Hatch.

'We gotta stop meeting down by the creeks.'

She ignored his remark, but was

studying him closely. 'I couldn't help hearing Harve trying to rile you. You don't give a damn about what people think of you, do you?'

He shrugged. 'Some people. Mostly, I take folks as I find 'em. If they don't take to me, makes no nevermind.'

'You can't have many friends!'

'Those I do, matter.'

She frowned, nodded slowly. 'Yes. I believe they would.'

'It's getting dark. You like me to stick around while you do your washing?'

'Thanks for the offer, but — no. I can take care of myself.'

'You didn't bring your rifle.'

She bristled. 'I don't depend on my gun all the time . . . like some people.'

He smiled crookedly, touched a hand to his hat-brim, started to move away.

'You're walking better.' As he turned, frowning slightly, she added, 'I believe you suffered a bad beating not long ago.'

'Seems a while back, but I'm about all better now.'

'Harve doesn't think so — or he wouldn't challenge you like that.'

He smiled and again touched a hand to his hat-brim. 'Thank you kindly. You better watch out, or I might add you to my short list.'

'Short list?'

'Of friends who matter.'

She watched him disappear into the dimness of the trees, then, as she began to sort her small load of washing, she smiled to herself.

'Who knows?' she murmured.

8

Dead Man's Hand

They were lucky: there was decent grass growing almost belly-deep in places in the foothills of the first of the fingerlike ranges. The place was known as Dead Man's Hand, not a particularly comforting name, but appropriate enough, the main range representing the heel of the hand while the five spurs fanned out from it like knobbly fingers.

It was between the first and second spurs that they came upon the grass.

'We'll rest 'em here for a few days,' Lindeen decided. 'Let 'em fill their bellies with sweetgrass before we push 'em on. Once clear of these hills, the grass doesn't look too promising, according to Landers.'

Skull Landers was the scout, the man who rode ahead, sometimes days in advance of the herd, spied out the country and the best route or diversions for grass and accessible water. He was a rawboned, lanky man with a skull-like face, sunken cheeks, and eyes set deep in their sockets. With the bones so prominent, thin lips peeling back from large teeth, his nickname was well-chosen. He didn't mind. Despite his cadaverous look and lonely job, Landers was a bright enough man, usually whistling some tune or humming a range ditty that took his fancy.

Maybe because his job was so lonely he liked to talk a lot when he was back in camp. Much of it was repetitious, the jokes old ones that had been told and retold, but he was such a likeable man that he always found an audience.

He favoured an old black-powder Hawken rifle, converted to take a long .45/.70 cartridge. He could drop a buffalo at 300 yards with it and legend had it that the gun broke his shoulder three times in the early days before he learned to grip it properly. There was a rumour that he once shot a running bear through the left eye at a hundred yards, not making much of the feat because he had aimed at the *right* eye.

Some of the men were trying to arrange a shooting match between Skull Landers and Meg Hatch but so far Lindeen had not agreed. Maybe he was saving such diversion until later, when they were nearing their destination, when the herd would be tired and cranky, hard to manage, like the trail-hands themselves. *Then* they would appreciate such a match, but with wages mounting and close to collection, there would be wild bets, too.

And arguments over payment once they hit the railhead. But that was all part and parcel of the whole shebang where trail driving was concerned.

Lindeen aimed to keep a lid on things while he could.

He sent Skull Landers on one more scouting trip while the herd was resting up and enjoying the sweet long grass.

'That drummer with the busted

wagon that you and some of the boys fixed, told me he hadn't seen much water north of here,' Lindeen explained. 'Maybe you better check it out, Skull, see if there's a creek or river we can swing to. Unless I go more to the east, which I don't want to do, because of the Indian problem, it'll be a long dry run. We've been lucky, only one stampede worthy of the name so far, but if there's not enough water . . . '

'Reckon there'll be some back in the canyons, chief.' Skull packed his old corncob pipe and lit up from a match that Lindeen struck and then applied to his own cheroot. 'Sandstone in there and basalt. Lots of hollows. There's bound to be pools.'

Lindeen nodded, but frowned. 'We've got over six thousand head, remember, Skull.'

'Yus, I know, chief, but I found an Apache kid about fourteen in there once, with a busted ankle. He'd been chasin' a wild pony he wanted. He told me there's a river in there. He used their word for 'river' but likely meant just a stream. I'll check it out.'

Lindeen was worried. That drummer had come down all the way from Bensonville and said they hadn't seen rain for weeks. Regular waterholes were little better than mud and a herd this size would suck the country dry of every drop available.

There was Brett's *remuda*, too. Thirsty horses were damned hard to work and a cantankerous horse not only made its rider bad-tempered but the mount's nervy actions could easily upset thirsty cattle.

'How're your horses holding up, Brett?'

'OK, so far. They were wild not so long ago. Used to surviving on less water than ranch-bred mounts.'

'Yes, I'd overlooked that.' Lindeen brightened. 'But just a word of warning. That drummer didn't paint a very happy picture of the trail we'll be following.'

'If anyone can sniff out water and

sweetgrass, it's old Skull, I reckon.'

That was the sort of thing Lindeen wanted to hear, but it blunted his edge of worry only a little — he had so much invested in this drive. If he didn't reach Bensonville at the right time, with the cows in prime condition — well, his plans for Hondo Basin were going to need drastic revision.

★　★　★

Skull returned just after sun-up on the second day and his news was good.

There was water in the canyon system of Dead Man's Hand.

'Yus, chief, that Apache kid was right, there's a kinda creek in there, or youse could call it a 'snake' water-hole.'

At Lindeen's quizzical look Skull grinned, showing gapped teeth grabbing his pipestem to keep it from falling, 'Long, windin' strip of water in a hollow the wind's carved in the rock. Stops here 'n' there, but shows up again after a few yards. Grass in a nearby canyon but she's a mite small, won't take even half the herd at a time.'

'We'll have to do it in shifts then. Let as many as we can in for a timed session, then drive 'em out and bring in the next lot,' Lindeen decided. He looked around at the sleepy-eyed men eating breakfast, but they were alert enough. 'Going to be a lot of hard work and long hours, men.'

'You mean we been havin' a picnic, so far?' said one of the drag riders. 'Hell, and here's me thinkin' all along, I was bustin' a gut!'

The others laughed, Lindeen right along with them.

'That's the attitude I like, Curly! It'll be tough, but there'll be a bonus for everyone when we get to the rail-head. On top of the normal one for bringing in the herd on schedule.'

That brightened the crew considerably and as they finished eating they mounted and rode out to relieve the nighthawks. Skull Landers helped himself to a third lot of warmed-over stew, glanced at Brett, who was draining his coffee mug, and spoke to Lindeen.

'Met a bunch of soldiers in there.'

Lindeen snapped his head up. 'In the canyons?'

Skull nodded, swallowed food before answering. 'Just a small squad — four men. They been huntin' some 'Patchies that broke outa the Mescalero reservation.'

'Damn! Renegade Indians are the last thing we need!'

'They say how many were on the loose, Skull?' asked Brett and Landers shook his head.

'Got the notion it weren't many. Some young bucks with a coupla bottles of tulapai is all. When it runs out and their hangovers are bad enough, they'll go back.'

'Where're the soldiers from?' Brett asked and Lindeen looked at him sharply.

Skull shrugged. 'Fort Winston, I'd reckon. That's nearest.'

'Still a damn long way off for such a

small squad to be wandering around independently, just after renegades,' Brett opined.

Lindeen frowned more deeply. 'Ye-es, does seem a little strange . . . They friendly enough, Skull?'

'Aw, yus, chief. Had a bottle of good rye — seal hadn't even been broke. I told 'em to look in on us if they got a chance, we'd return their hospitality. Hope that was all right, chief?'

'I hope so, too, Skull.' Lindeen turned as Brett said:

'Long way for soldiers without an officer to carry a sealed bottle of whiskey, from Fort Winston.'

Lindeen frowned. 'That's right! See Harve on the way out and tell him to double up on the wing riders, and we'll do the same with nighthawks when we bed down.'

Brett nodded and smiled thinly as he walked away: Harve Ricketts would love taking orders from him.

* * *

But it did no good.

The herd was pushed into the edge of the canyon country and there was hell's own job holding back those that were waiting to be taken in for water. It was made even harder because the extra nighthawks were men who had had the chore last night and were without their full measure of sleep.

Maybe they were slack, dozing in the saddle, but right on moonset, an hour or so past midnight, mystery riders hit the herd.

They came in shooting and yelling, and might have been the renegades the soldiers were hunting. All the war cries and gunfire set the herd on its feet, bawling and lowing, horns clashing, raking hide, starting angry, hurt bellowing. The unrest spread like a wildfire fanned by a high north wind.

In seconds they were ready to stampede.

It was renegades' tactics: hit the herd like a tornado, set it stampeding, then cut out a few steers for themselves and leave the chaos for the trail men to sort out.

In the narrow canyons, with hundreds of panicking cattle jumping each other, jammed tight as they all tried to turn and get through the crush at the entrances at the same time, it was mighty dangerous, for riders *and* the herd.

Brett heard one rider scream, whipped his head around in time to see the man bloodily crushed against the sandstone wall by the press of spooked cows. The horse reared, pawing the night, but long horns raked its belly, slicing it open like a gutted bass ready for the campfire.

Brett had his hands full, kicking, slashing with the stiff coils of his lariat, trying to protect his sorrel. The horse's eyes were rolling, nostrils flared and snorting. Mucus sprayed over his face and hands. His soothing words were lost in the bedlam. The guns had stopped but it made no difference at this stage; the herd was loose in a fury of panic and once clear of the canyons would scatter to hell and gone, in all out stampede.

And that was what happened. Once the beasts were free of the canyon, almost every one of them bearing scars from rocks or horns, those still on their feet, who had not been trampled down, began to *run*. Brett had never seen so many cattle running so fast. His trail-driving experience was limited, but he knew this was no ordinary stampede. This was one for the history books!

The herd took off, scattering, trampling what little grass there was, thundering recklessly through the scarce waterholes on the flats, turning them into muddy morasses. Some broke legs and went down, to be trampled by those following. The ones in front were simply *moving* fast, going *anywhere*, it didn't matter which direction they took or what stood in their path, they just had to *go*!

The thundering herd went straight through any obstacles — or over them. It would take a miracle to stop them.

Riders sweated and cursed until they were hoarse. Two men at least went down, never to rise again, their mounts pulped into raw mincemeat as well. Lindeen roared for the men to get the cook wagons and supply wagons out of the way but they were only partly successful.

One cook wagon, with a built-in, coal-fired oven at the rear for biscuits and flapjacks, lifted into the air as cows battered it, overturned it, and within seconds it was ablaze. The terrified team fought the tangled harness, dragging the blazing pyre behind, spreading fire until they collapsed, exhausted. This added to the terror of the herd as it swirled around it, or, in a few cases, through it.

It was a night out of hell and seemed to have no end.

And when at last it did end, the comparison with Hell was fully justified.

Four men dead, six more with injuries bad enough to incapacitate them, almost a hundred head of cattle down, strewn across the flats, choking the canyons and draws, just as many again missing. The bawling agony and cries of anguish filled the darkness like lost souls.

Brett's *remuda* had fared well enough, the recently wild horses' survival instincts were still strong, causing them to veer away from the main stampede and seek sanctuary amongst the draws and dry washes. But he reckoned at least twenty or more were missing. Many of the others had injuries that were bad enough to keep them from working for a few days at least.

'Need to go looking in there, boss,' he told the harassed Lindeen, gesturing to the canyons. 'They'll find places we'll never be able to get to and — '

'You're on your own, Brett,' Lindeen snapped. 'Can't spare any men, but I agree, we need those horses. Go see if you can pick up their tracks. Later I may be able to send someone to help.'

Brett wheeled the sorrel with its many, though thankfully minor, wounds, and lifted the mount towards the shadows and clefts of the canyon country.

He was a good way into the twisting canyons in an hour. As the stars faded he rested his mount by a rock pool, drank deeply himself, waiting for daylight. He was surprised to find his hand shaking as he built a cigarette, realized all the exertion and rush of excitement was leaving him now: the shakes were the natural aftermath.

But there would be plenty of tension yet; he had to find those missing horses. As it was, the herd was going to take days to round up and there were still a lot of miles to go before they reached the railhead.

It would be touch and go whether Lindeen would arrive on time. If he missed the meat-house train . . . well, not only Lindeen would lose out, but every rancher in the Hondo Basin who had cows in the big herd as well. Lindeen might weather it and be able to make another try next season, but most of those small spreads would go under.

He let the sorrel have its head once

daybreak washed a little light down into the canyons. There were many shadows, but red-tinged light crept down the walls and gradually turned yellow and then into the spreading brightness of a full day forming.

The sorrel's ears were upright and working hard, flicking this way and that, nostrils twitching, brief rumbles — unborn whinnies — sounded from within the big chest, which was streaked with gashes and dried blood from last night's terror.

He smelled the other mounts. Brett urged him on quietly, nudging with his heels, squeezing with his thighs but not hard enough to take control; the sorrel was in charge now and, suddenly realizing it, whinnied and increased its pace.

There was fresh dung here and there — fresh as having been deposited last night, anyway — and twice Brett heard answering whinnies. But it was hard to tell where they came from, echoing as they did from this maze of rock walls.

Then they came to a set of rock pools, placed like a triangle. There were wet hoofprints on the rocks around two of them, drying fast as the sun gained heat.

He couldn't be sure which way they led because they had dried by now, but the sorrel barely hesitated, weaved through a snaking passage and came out into brush and a small stand of trees.

Brett hauled rein and slid his rifle out of its scabbard, just as a voice from above him echoed around, with the words:

'Howdy, Brett. Been waitin' for you. Hope you've brought our money, you son of a bitch!'

9

One Man Posse

Brett recognized Yank Bilby's womanish voice, even though the sandstone threw the echoes back at a deeper pitch.

He sat the sorrel and started to turn slowly, seeing the movement above and to his left on a small ledge with a round end. Yank stood there, holding a rifle pointed down at him. He was wearing army trousers with a blue stripe down each side. Grey suspenders held the trousers up over a long-sleeved cotton-knit shirt.

'Ripley and Boots'd be with you. Who's the fourth 'soldier'?'

Yank looked thrown slightly, then the rifle barrel jerked. 'You'll find out. Lift your hands shoulder high and use your legs to march that crowbait between that grey rock and the yaller one opposite. *Move!*'

Brett obeyed and found there was a clearing amongst the trees here with three men sitting on logs, passing a whiskey bottle around. Ripley, Boots Skene — and the third man? Vaguely familiar . . . *Hell, yeah!*

'You looked better with your Vandyck.' Brett shifted his gaze to Ripley as the sorrel halted. 'You boys've been busy. Never heard of anyone escaping from the territorial prison before. Then joining the army.'

Ripley gave that tight, clenched-teeth grin, pleased at Brett's words. 'Told that damn judge they'd never hold me. Climb down, Brett. Just don't let your hands wander anywhere near your guns.'

Brett dismounted and Boots stepped behind him, lifted his Colt out of the holster, rammed it in his own belt. Then he took the rifle and let out a long breath.

'*Now* I feel better.' He shoved Brett and he stumbled, trying to retain balance. Boots prodded him with the rifle barrel. 'Set on the nearest log, hands on your knees — an' *don't move 'em!*'

Once again Brett obeyed and Boots moved around to join Ripley and Dutchy. Yank arrived from his ledge a minute or so later. They sat there staring at him.

'You've got all the guns. You can open the meeting now. But first, what happened to the soldiers who owned them uniforms you're wearing?'

'What d'you think?' said Ripley without an iota of interest in his voice. He took a swig of the whiskey, looked at the bottle and then at Brett. 'That scout of Lindeen's sure likes his booze. Couldn't stop him talkin' after a couple swigs of this stuff.'

'Figured you used it to find out about the herd.'

'And who was workin' the *remuda!*' cut in Yank in his high voice.

'Couldn't b'lieve our luck,' Tad Ripley said, still with that trademark grin. 'Found out you were workin' for Lindeen but figured we'd have to go all the way to Hondo Basin to get to you. 'Stead, Lindeen brings you right to us!'

'There's no money, Tad,' Brett told him flatly, and the grin faded. The others tensed, too.

'Now you just better give that matter a little more thought, Brett, *amigo*! Yank passed you the four bags and I seen you myself stuff 'em in that big canvas sack we brung along just for that purpose! Buzz was shot by Bolan an' his deputies, an' you nailed Stormy, so it was only you come runnin' to the getaway mounts.' Ripley stood abruptly, face hard, fingers on his right hand flexing as he held the hand above his gun butt. 'And you were carryin' that sack, slung it over your saddlehorn an' lit out like the Devil hisself had his red-hot fork up your ass!' He started forward. 'Now don't you try to tell me *there ain't no money*!' He shouted the last words.

His gun was in his hand now and he

thumbed back the hammer, knocked Brett's hat off and rammed the barrel between the man's eyes.

'Tell me what you done with it or I'll blow the top of your head off!'

Brett's belly was knotted up and he felt his gorge rising, but he swallowed and somehow managed to keep a steady voice as he looked up at the crazy-angry outlaw.

'You kill me, Tad, you won't find out anything.'

Ripley had obviously already thought of that, and the knowledge that he had made an empty threat only fed his anger. With a growl deep in the back of his throat he swiped the gun barrel across Brett's head, knocking him off the log.

It was a glancing blow but Brett saw stars and his ears rang as a thin trickle of blood ran from his split scalp. Dazed, he blinked, put up a hand to the throbbing place and grunted as Ripley kicked him in the right thigh. Brett fell sideways, took another boot in the back between the shoulders, and then a kick to the back of his head slammed his face into the grass.

Ripley leaned down, prodding painfully with the gun barrel. Then he placed the blade foresight against Brett's right eye socket.

'I'll have both your eyes out on your cheeks if you don't — *gimme* — *my* — *money*!'

'Hey, Tad. It's *our* money,' corrected Yank Bilby. He threw up a protective arm as the Colt swung towards him, thinking he was about to be shot. 'Jeez, hold up, Tad!'

He came mighty close to dying right then. It was only by a powerful effort of will that Ripley refrained from dropping the hammer. The murderous look was still on his face and Bilby swallowed audibly.

'I — I only meant — '

'Shut up!' After one lingering glare Ripley turned back to Brett, who was now sitting on the log again, holding his head, the world swaying behind a curtain of bright, blinking lights. 'You think I'm bluffin', Brett?'

'No, Tad. And I'm not lying.'

Ripley had to make another big effort not to shoot or at least to gunwhip Brett senseless. His eyes narrowed. 'I say you are!' The gritted smile appeared briefly. 'Now that's fightin' words to the Brett McCabe I know. You wanna try for your gun? Boots can toss it within a yard of where you're sittin'. All you have to do is pick it up.'

Brett smiled crookedly, without mirth. 'I'll pass this time, Tad. You got my permission to call me a liar and I swear I won't kill you — today.'

Ripley laughed. 'Hey, *amigo*, ain't you figured it yet? Today's all you got. For you, there' ain't no tomorrow.'

Brett managed a shrug, wound up like a clock spring inside. 'And for you, there' ain't no bank loot.'

Ripley swore. 'Goddamnit! You gonna keep this up?'

'Just 'til sundown.' Brett knew he had to be careful: Ripley would push just so far and suddenly he would snap — and to hell with the consequences.

'Yeah, well sundown could come mighty early for you!' Tad jerked the Colt at Brett. 'C'mon, for Chris'sakes! We busted outa jail when Dutchy here told us you was still alive. Bolan said you was dead, out in the badlands, an' we believed him. What Dutchy said was you threw him off a train.'

'And I'd do it again.' Brett knew that he must just keep them talking, riled up some, so they'd concentrate on the money while he tried to think of a way out of this. Because if he couldn't, Brett knew Ripley would kill him. Even if he told the truth, he was still likely to die.

Ripley studied Brett and suddenly made his decision. 'Yank — Boots. Tie the sonuver up. Hands *an'* feet.'

'We gonna take him with us?' Boots asked, puzzled.

'Bury what's left of him?' queried Yank.

'Aw, I dunno. Might just leave him. Oughta be enough left to feed a couple coyotes.' The smile came again. 'That got you worried, Brett?'

'Not yet.'

Ripley laughed. 'See, you still got your sense of humour! Well, that'll soon change. Dutchy, you can earn a share of this. You told us what that greaser maniac done to your pard in Sonora one time. Reckon you can recollect the details? You can practise first on Brett a bit if you want . . . just till you get it right.'

Dutchy didn't look too sure. 'I dunno, Tad. It — it turned my stomach. Dunno as I could do the same.'

'Then you might's well leave.' No grin on Ripley's face now. 'But you won't get a red cent!'

Dutchy ran a tongue around his lips, glanced at Brett. 'How — how much we talkin' about?'

'Hell, I dunno.' We never had time to count it. But there was four heavy bags. When they were all in the one sack Brett was draggin' his tail and near busted a gut liftin' it up an' over his saddle horn. That's how come he was last man ridin' out, just fast enough to dodge posse bullets.'

Dutchy's eyes glittered. 'I — I can remember what to do.'

'Right! Now what you want?'

'Some slivers of wood for under his fingernails and a — a bigger sharp stake for . . . ' He just nodded to Brett's lower regions.

'Jesus Christ!' breathed Boots and Yank pursed his lips doubtfully.

Ripley laughed, turned to Brett, nudging him roughly with a boot toe. 'Mebbe we don't need to do nothin, eh? You start talkin' just any time you feel like it, Brett, ol' pard.'

That was what shook Brett: it was too late now! He should never have tried to rile Ripley — now the man wouldn't believe anything he said . . .

Not until Brett was broken and so close to death that Ripley would have no option *but* to believe what, by that time, he would be frantic to tell him . . .

Then there was a booming thunder

like a crack of doom and something thrummed in its passage through the trees. Small branches splintered and erupted with a shower of leaves, almost drowning the voice that yelled, 'Go round! Go round! Cut 'em off or we'll lose 'em!'

There was a clatter of hoofs, a couple of whinnies and by then the outlaws were scattering for their mounts tethered just inside the line of trees.

'Posse!' Dutchy bawled, leading the exodus.

A six-gun banged in four rapid shots, lead screaming off the rocks. The big thunder crashed again and this time a hatful of sandstone sprayed off a high boulder near the trees, where the outlaws were leaping into their saddles.

Ripley paused long enough to snap two shots at the bound Brett. Lead kicked dirt into his face and eyes. He heard the rumble of racing horses crashing through the brush and then the outlaws were gone, six-guns cracking, bullets seeking them.

In moments a half-dozen riderless horses that Brett recognized as belonging to the *remuda* raced through the camp and slowed at the line of trees, whinnying, snapping at each other as they collided briefly, looking bewildered.

Another horse appeared, with a rider: Skull Landers, grinning and trying to whistle at the same time. He was clutching his big Hawken rifle in one hand and held a smoking Colt in the other. A second pistol was rammed into his belt.

'Cavalry's here!'

Brett spat some grit and tried to grin. 'Only thing you needed was a bugle, Skull.'

Skull grinned and knelt, taking his Bowie knife and cutting Brett's wrist bonds.

*   *   *

'Skull used his head. He'd come across seven or eight of the *remuda*, heard

156

Ripley cussing me out. Those narrow canyons echo to hell and gone. He set the horses running at the camp. They thought it was a posse charging in.'

Lindeen listened to Brett's story and Skull, standing nearby with Harve Ricketts and Chuck Iles, shrugged as all eyes turned to him.

'Just had a spur of the moment notion.'

'Keep on having 'em, Skull,' Brett told him with a grin and offering his hand. 'It's fine with me.'

Skull chuckled, shaking hands briefly. 'It sure looked like you was about to be dressed out like a plucked chicken.'

'More like a pig,' Harve dropped in, just to be his usual sociable self. 'Well, he's back now; might's well get on back to work. Unless Brett wants to tell us about the money . . . ?'

'There's no money, Harve. None at all.'

Harve scowled. Lindeen motioned to Brett to stay as the others moved off, Harve talking with Skull, Chuck ambling along behind in his usual agreeable manner.

Brett took the cheroot Lindeen offered, and the light. Blowing smoke, the trail boss, red-eyed and as dirty and weary as any of his men, said, 'Mebbe I know a trifle more about your background than the others, Brett . . . '

Lindeen's stare was steady but Brett met and held it. The trail boss nodded gently. 'Likely I have no right to say this but — they were men from Telford, weren't they?'

Brett didn't want this conversation, but he owed a lot to Lindeen; the man didn't realize just how big a chance he had given Brett by taking him on as a wrangler. He didn't realize how much Brett appreciated the gesture, even allowing that Brett had saved Lindeen's life.

'You've got every right. Yeah. Last place I knew 'em was at Telford — if I can put it that way.'

Lindeen smiled thinly. 'Very neat and satisfactory. But I understood those men had been captured and sent to prison for life?'

'Ripley found a way to bust out.'

'Are they here for any specific purpose?'

Brett sighed, nodded. 'They're after some money they think I have.'

'And you don't?'

'No.'

There was that steady, studying gaze again, then Lindeen nodded briefly. 'Good enough. Soon as you feel up to it, get the *remuda* together and give me a head count. I can see we've lost some.'

'I'll try to make it as accurate as possible . . . and thanks again for — understanding.'

'*You* don't seem to understand, Brett: I'm here, alive. I wouldn't be if you hadn't happened along that night.'

'Don't feel like I did anything out of the ordinary.'

'You're not standing where I am.' Lindeen clapped him on the shoulder before turning away towards one of the mostly restored chuck wagons. 'Have some coffee before you go back to work.'

It was strong, freshly made. Both men had an extra mugful.

'The men are edgy,' Lindeen said abruptly. 'I guess it's usual enough at this stage of a big drive. I'll bet some of them even welcomed that stampede just for a break in routine. But it's been a hard few days rounding up the herd, and having to destroy so many injured cows doesn't go down well with most of the hands. They're getting impatient to reach the end of the trail — and I have to admit that I am, too.'

Brett nodded. 'There've been a few fights, I've noticed. Some pretty damn vicious.'

'That's what I'm talking about. The men are touchy and when trouble explodes, they go all out regardless. We've enough injuries now without brawls adding to them.'

'If we had a troupe of dancing gals . . . '

Lindeen smiled wistfully. 'And don't think I haven't wished for that!' He looked suddenly thoughtful. 'But some sort of . . . diversion is needed, even if it delays the drive for a few hours.'

'You could set up that shooting match between Skull and Meg Hatch. I've heard some of the crew talking about it.'

'Ye-es. Only thing is there'll be betting and that might breed even more aggravation — '

'You'll get bad losers anywhere. Won't come to a head until you pay 'em off and it's settling-up time.'

The trail boss nodded slowly. 'That's so. I'll give it some thought. But if I decide to stage it, it'll have to be well away from the herd. I can't take a chance on the gunfire unsettling them again.'

'Skull ought to be able to find a place. That's if the girl will agree to the contest.'

'Brett, you are just too damn smart for me.' Lindeen laughed briefly at the surprise on the other's battered face. 'I mean, you can see too many 'ifs' and 'buts'. I savvy now why Sheriff Casmeier complained about my raising so many questions when I was booking the holding pens.' He stubbed out his cheroot. 'I'll figure something out.'

Brett rinsed his mug in the keg of water kept for that purpose and hung it on a nail. As he limped back towards the rope corrals to check on his sorrel, he saw Meg Hatch riding to cut off a steer that had broken away from the main herd. She was good, seemed a part of the racing white horse, its mane and tail streaming, as she weaved and dogged the steer, blocking its every manoeuvre effortlessly. She used her rope sparingly, clouting it twice behind one ear before the steer gave up and trotted back to join the main herd. When she eased back in the saddle he saw the smile of satisfaction on her tanned face. He waved his hat to draw her attention. 'You want a job on the *remuda*, just say the word.'

Her smile faded, then returned halfway. She hesitated, then waved before riding back to her place on the wing.

10

Targets

Harve Ricketts was watching Brett. That was obvious enough, the way the man found so many chores or checks to make within sight of where the wrangler happened to be working. He tried not to make clear what he was about but Brett was a man used to keeping an eye out for anything that might endanger his liberty — or his life.

Eventually Brett's apparent aloofness got the better of Harve, and he appeared out of the brush when the wrangler was watering some of the convalescent horses at the sandstone well just within the canyons.

'Your friends ain't come back, huh?'

Brett looked up slowly, although he had been aware of Ricketts's presence for some time. 'What 'friends' would they be, Harve?'

'Come on! You know who I mean — and you know how Skull loves to talk, can't help himself.'

'Yeah, I've noticed that. But how's it affect me?'

Harve Ricketts sighed. 'Like to do things the hard way, don't you?'

'Like all cards on the table where I can read 'em.'

'Uh-huh. OK. Skull heard some things before he busted in to save your neck. Sounded to him, and me since he told me, like you knew those *hombres* and owed 'em some money.'

'That how it sounded to you, huh?'

Ricketts's face coloured. His hands on the saddle horn had white knuckles. 'Goddamn you, Brett! Don't you smartmouth me! I've told you before.'

'In one ear and out the other, Harve. And don't bother saying there's nothing in between to stop it happening. I've heard it a thousand times from *hombres* just like you, with no imagination.'

164

The ramrod's eyes narrowed and he started to swing down from his horse. He checked when Brett turned to face him fully, boots spread, right hand close to his holstered Colt, which replaced the one Boots had taken. Harve settled back into leather but he looked mighty riled.

'O-K! All along, I've had you figured for a man on the run, Brett. By my reckonin', some of your old pards've caught up with you and they want somethin' you owe 'em.'

'I don't owe anyone anything, Harve. Make a point of not being in debt, moneywise or obligation-wise.'

'Well, ain't you Mr Goody-Goody! Like hell!' Harve wagged a finger down at Brett. 'I ain't dumb. I can figure things and I reckon I've got this deal figured right.'

'You're entitled to your opinion, Harve, but what good will it do you, even if you are right?'

Ricketts smiled thinly, leaned forward, almost confidentially. 'That's yet to be settled, but you're one agin four, accordin' to Skull. Two agin four'd make better odds — and better sense.'

'You got that part about 'better odds' right. Not the rest of it.'

Harve smiled without humour. 'Aw, you just ain't thought it through yet. I mean, s'pose I went to Lindeen an' told him what I know?'

'What you *think* you know, Harve. And s'pose Lindeen already knows?'

That rocked the ramrod and he sat his saddle, frowning deeply, genuinely surprised. 'Well — that ain't likely.'

Brett shrugged, started to gather the hackamore ropes, the horses coming easily to his tugs now that they had had their fill of cool water.

'Is it?' Ricketts insisted.

'I'm busy, Harve, got another batch of broncs to water. Go see Lindeen and find out for yourself.'

He led the horses past the ramrod, and began to walk back to where Chuck Iles was holding the rest of the *remuda* with the help of a couple of cowhands who were recovering slowly from injuries received during the stampede.

Ricketts watched him sourly, wondering what had gone wrong. It had seemed so simple: make Brett cut him in for a share of whatever money was involved — and it would be substantial if these four renegades Skull saw were willing to torture and kill Brett — or he would go tell Lindeen, who was no fool . . .

Nah! Harve said to himself. *Lindeen wouldn't have no truck with an outlaw! He don't know nothin' — but maybe I'll tell him.*

Still, there had been some kind of strange connection between the two of them when Lindeen had first brought Brett back to Chain. Maybe Harve better look into this some more before he tipped his hand.

★   ★   ★

There was another vicious brawl after supper that night, and a knife was drawn.

Only Harve Ricketts's fast intervention kept murder from being done.

It had started between two point riders over a cup of coffee. Red had inadvertently added sugar to Cato's cup when he had gone to get the drinks, his mind on something else. Cato had had a bad day, was suffering with a massive toothache but refused to let the cook pull the rotten tooth. His horse had gone lame up in the hills and he had had a long, painful walk back, every step driving electric shocks through his jawbone.

There was beefsteak for supper again and it was *tough*. He couldn't chew properly, had to slice and cut and hack the meat into small portions that he could swallow. It gave him indgestion. Then Red had offered to get him another cup of coffee, because the first one had cooled.

'Goddamit! You know I don't take sugar!' roared Cato, lurching to his feet. This was the last straw. 'Sugar gettin' into that tooth of mine'll only make it worser!'

'Hell, Cat, I'm sorry. Din' think, just dumped in four spoonfuls.'

By then the agony-ridden Cato's rage was burning bright and it erupted when he tossed the hot coffee onto Red's freckled shirtfront. 'Goddamn block-head!'

That was it. Red, screaming blasphemies, launched himself at Cato and they wrecked half the supper camp as they brawled and trampled their way around, smashing at each other, not only with their fists but anything they could snatch up — including a blazing stick from the cookfire, a pan of greasy water (hot), a trail oven's iron lid, a muddy boot drying out by the fire and, last of all, Cato's knife, glinting in the firelight.

Cheering, roaring men suddenly went silent as Cato slashed savagely at Red's throat. Red jumped back, white as a maiden's nightdress, bruises, blood and freckles standing out against the corpse-pale skin as the blade whistled past within an inch of his jugular.

169

'Hell almighty!'

Cato lunged again and Red looked wildly around for some weapon to defend himself with. Then Harve Ricketts stepped in, swung an iron skillet against Cato's head and drove the man to his knees. Harve hit him again, stretching him out, and Red breathed a sigh of relief, shaking noticeably.

'Th-thanks, Harve . . . I . . . '

Harve laid him out, too, alongside Cato, with a single swipe of the skillet. He flung it away, glaring around at the silent trail crew.

'That's the last fight I want to see in this camp! Next man gets a bullet through his foot and my boot in his ass — right outta here! You damn idiots savvy?'

There were sullen murmurs and Lindeen came and stood beside the big ramrod.

'I'll back Harve all the way,' he said. 'Dammit, men! We're behind to blazes! We don't get this herd in on time, you don't see any wages — that was our agreement. Now settle down and help me get these cows up the trail to Bensonville. The bonuses still stand, but anyone who starts more trouble can forget about ever seeing one dime more than his wages.'

The crew shuffled off, murmuring, heads together. They hadn't liked that ultimatum. They had all been bitching in some way since the stampede: the workload had increased because of injuries laying several men low. These men had been accused of malingering, even by some who had been their pards previously on the drive, up until now. The strain was beginning to take its toll.

Lindeen caught Brett's eye. 'I think that competition better be arranged. Tell Skull I'd like to see him. Oh, and Meg and her father, too.'

Brett nodded; something sure had to be done before they had a major mutiny on their hands.

'Boss,' he said suddenly, pointing to

the unconscious Cato, whose mouth was hanging open. 'If you've got your pliers handy . . . ?'

Lindeen frowned, then smiled. 'Of course! Andy, get my pliers, and we'll get rid of at least one source of trouble.'

'If I was you, boss,' said Andy when he returned with the tool. 'I'd stand well back when Cat comes round again.'

Everyone suddenly discovered things that had to be done elsewhere and Brett and Lindeen found themselves alone with the two unconscious men.

'Care to sit on his head or something?' Lindeen asked, snapping the pliers open and closed.

'Wouldn't care to, but guess someone has to — dammit!'

Milo Hatch was against the shooting competition but he gave no real reason.

'You know I got Meg to shoot them bottles before just to let the men know they wouldn't get close to her without running the risk of stopping a bullet — and it worked. I got cows in this herd, too, Lindeen, and she's my daughter, so I figure I'm entitled to a say.'

'You are.'

'Well, we've lost almost a week and I don't mind tellin' you I'm edgy about us makin' Bensonville by the due date. We miss them buyers, I can't afford to let my herd go for peanuts! I say to hell with the games, get on with the drive.'

'Nothing I'd like better, Milo, but you've seen the state of the men. They've worked damned hard and with some of them still mostly out of action for the big chores, they'll have to work harder still to get us along the trail. They not only need a diversion, they deserve it.' The trail boss turned to the silent Skull Landers who was quietly humming some ditty to himself. 'Skull? You willing?'

'Sure would like to see if I can outshoot Miss Hatch.' He grinned at the girl who was sitting on a log, sipping coffee. She hadn't so far joined in the discussion. 'You game, miss?'

Meg lowered the coffee cup, glanced at her father. 'Nice of someone to consult me,' she said a little stiffly but took the edge off the words by half-smiling. 'Skull, if you can shoot that Hawken of yours downwind so I'm not deafened by the blast, I'll be happy to satisfy your curiosity.'

Skull's grin widened. 'I can do that!'

'Now just a minute, Meg! I've already vetoed this.'

'But it's not you doing the shooting, Pa, and Mr Lindeen is right. The men are dragging their tails, if you'll excuse the expression, half-asleep on their feet, and we all know how short their tempers are. They *do* need some kind of diversion to break the tension. I feel it's my duty to help if I can.'

Milo Hatch tightened his lips, and everyone there knew then where the girl got the same habit when she was feeling put out: the resemblance was remarkable, even allowing for the difference in ages — and sex.

'You have not yet reached your majority, girl!'

'It's not a matter for the calendars, Pa, that sort of thing — you told me so yourself. 'Maturity' is the word you used, I believe. I feel I'm at least halfway there.'

'Dammit, don't you throw my words back in my face!' He was on his feet now, glaring around at the men present: Lindeen, Skull, and Brett who was silently smoking in the background. 'What's he doing here anyway? Is he going to shoot, too?'

'Nope.' That was Brett's sole contribution to the meeting so far and he stood up now. 'I'll leave you to it.'

They watched him go, each gathering his thoughts.

'We'll need to find somewhere where the shooting won't alarm the cattle,' Lindeen said. Hatch turned and stormed off, muttering. 'I'm sorry if this causes a rift between you and your father, Meg, but — '

'Oh, he'll come round. He's a little

too protective, doesn't like me being the centre of attention with so many men around. I — I'm not doing it for that. I really believe we need to give the crew something to ease the strain.'

'Appreciate your agreement, Meg. You and Skull will have to find somewhere to stage it, and the sooner the better.' Lindeen looked over to where Brett was arranging his gear for nighthawk duty. 'Brett, is there anywhere in that canyon country where we could stage the competition?'

'I dunno, boss, but those fellers who gave me a hard time might still be hanging about.'

The trail boss smothered a curse — in deference to Meg's presence. 'It would be ideal in there. The high walls will contain the sound so it doesn't spook the herd.'

Brett nodded slowly. 'I guess maybe Skull put those *hombres* on the run. They won't want to hang around so many men with guns. How you gonna decide who sees it and who stays to watch the herd?'

'Short straws.'

'We can do two shows,' Meg offered, glancing at Skull. 'So everyone can see. Otherwise there'll be more trouble than ever if some have to miss out entirely.'

Lindeen agreed. Brett shouldered his saddle rig and walked across to the *remuda* to select a horse for his spell at nighthawk duty.

He hoped Ripley had cleared this neck of the woods by now! Hoped like hell he had . . .

★   ★   ★

Just within the foothills, where the canyons started, there was a place that would be ideal for the shooting competition.

It was in a grassy hollow, a sort of shallow, natural amphitheatre, where spectators could sit on the slopes and look down on the actual target area.

There were sandstone and basalt walls rising on two sides, trees and brush on the other two, all slightly below the level of the plains where the herd was now swiftly recovering from the ordeal of their stampede.

Lindeen had made up his bundle of straws, twenty-five long, eight short, to see who went first. Men were already making bets as to who would win the shoot-out.

'I've worked with Skull before — seen him make shots you wouldn't believe. Some from hossback, flat out. My money goes on him.'

'How much you wanna put up?'

'Hell, I dunno how much pay we'll collect, but — aw, I reckon I'll put a sawbuck on Skull.'

'Piker! But, OK. I'll cover it — and add another five that Meg beats him, five targets outta six.'

'You're loco! She ain't that good!'

'Can I buy in? I'll take Handy's bet. That gal's gonna whup the ass offa Skull. See how much talkin' he does after that!'

Lindeen couldn't stop this kind of

thing and it bothered him; no matter what the outcome, some of these men were going to lose a large portion of their trail pay before they even reached railhead.

And once the wages were paid and collection time came round — well, he hoped that Casmeier was as good as he reckoned; trouble was a dead certainty.

Meg and Skull didn't know about the betting right now, although they knew it would take place in some way before and during the contest.

They scouted around the small amphitheatre and both agreed it couldn't be better.

'Set up targets along that ripple in the ground,' said Skull, pointing to a grass-covered ridge rising almost all the way across one corner.

'Ye-es. It's a good position, can be seen from any part of the slopes. What're we going to shoot at?'

'Cookie oughta have some cans we can use, mebbe some more essence bottles. But we can get pieces of bark and paint some dots or squares or circles on 'em.'

'We don't want to make it too easy.'

'Oh-ho! Miss Confidence, huh? Well, how about some matchboxes, or cigarette papers stuck to a rock . . . ?'

'If we're careful about ricochets. There'll be an audience all round, remember. What was that?'

Meg broke, off, suddenly looking alert, staring past Skull's shoulder.

Puzzled, he hipped in the saddle. 'What?'

'I thought — I thought I saw something moving behind those bushes — Oh! Over in the trees! There *is* a horse moving around!'

'Well, there's still a few of the *remuda* loose in here.'

As he spoke Skull heard a horse crash through the line of brush to his right, and horsehoes clunking on the rocks at the foot of the basalt wall.

Heart hammering a little faster than usual, Skull reached for his rifle.

He hoped those horses didn't have riders!

11

Deadly Message

It was a dull sound, like a drunk clumping erratically up the stairs at the other end of a passage.

Harve Ricketts wasn't even sure he had heard anything out of the ordinary but when he saw his mount's ears standing straight up and the horse looking in the direction the sound had come from, he decided he must've heard something.

The ramrod was working with three other cowhands on the edge of the flats where they had built a small but fierce campfire. In a temporary brush corral they had eight cows, all of them with hip injuries that had either destroyed or partly obliterated the Chain brand. This had been checked carefully by other owners of cattle in the herd, making sure the brand *was* Chain's and not someone else's. There were two other branding fires going, way back across the flats; other Hondo Basin ranchers were renewing damaged brands on stock.

As Andy Stein prepared to plant the hot iron on the hide of the cow being held down, Harve asked, 'You fellers, hear that sound just then?'

Andy, fighting the cow which was bellowing in his ear, shook his head, but Tex McClaren said he thought he heard something, not quite a rumble, but something like that.

'Mebbe a loose rock fallin' in there.' He jerked his head towards the distant foothills.

'Be a damn big rock!' Harve allowed but Bob Merry, dragging in another protesting beast, said he hadn't heard anything out of the ordinary.

Harve saw the downed cow branded and jumped back as Andy released it and Bob moved in with the next one. They threw the beast, expertly whipping short rope lengths around all four legs, but even so Bob caught a kick in the ribs that snagged his breath and spoiled his burst of imaginative swearing because he had to stop every couple of syllables to gasp in pain.

They branded the remaining cows and Bob and Andy let them out of the corral, bunching and driving them back towards the main herd. Tex McClaren wanted to know if he should remove the brush corral or leave it for any other cows they might find with spoiled brands.

'Knock it down. We're about through. Once they get this shootin'-match over with we'll be on the trail to Bensonville again.'

While Tex began the demolition of the corral, Harve mounted, still looking towards the foothills.

'Comin', Harve?' Tex was mounted now, sweating, looking forward to hot coffee and biscuits back at camp.

'Be along. Make sure Andy enters them alterations in the tally book.'

Tex waved, turned his mount and

rode off. But he looked back once and was surprised to see Harve riding towards the foothills, his rifle butt resting on his thigh now.

*   *   *

The day was almost done and the men who had pulled nighthawk duty grumpily ate an early supper, criticizing the cook for this or that: steak too fresh, steak too tough, not cooked enough, cooked too damn much, coffee too hot, coffee too cold, coffee too weak, biscuits burnt . . .

'Get the hell outta here an' do your gripin' to the stars, you sons of bitches!' growled the cook, brandishing a heavy soup ladle when he had had enough.

The nighthawks were laughing now they had gotten a rise out of Cookie and he ran at them swearing, stumbling — and the rest of the camp knew he had been sucking on the essence bottles again; no wonder the Sunday duff had

had little flavour to it.

'Where's Harve?' Lindeen asked a little testily, coming out of his canvas shelter after checking the tally books and other necessary papers for the drive.

'Was headin' for them foothills last I seen of him,' Tex McClaren said, tugging off his boots with a sigh and massaging aching feet.

'The foothills? What was he doing going there?'

Tex shrugged and Andy said, 'Might've been lookin' for Skull an' Miss Meg.'

Brett, near by with a plate of food, felt himself stiffen and snapped his head up. 'They're not back yet?'

'Ain't seen 'em.'

'Why wasn't I told?' Lindeen snapped. He had just opened his mouth to berate such a thoughtless crew when Bob Merry called, 'Couple riders comin' in now. Must be them.'

But it wasn't.

Leastways, only *one* of the missing pair, shepherded in by Harve Ricketts.

'The hell's wrong with Skull?' someone

said as the shadowy riders entered the camp.

The ramrod was riding alongside Skull Landers's mount but the scout definitely looked strange; he was sitting ramrod straight in the saddle, but his head was hanging, chin on chest, his hands in his lap, reins looped loosely.

Brett was on his feet in an instant, running towards the pair, and Milo Hatch, coming back from washing up after the day's work, called in a shaky voice: 'Where's Meg? Where's my daughter?'

Harve stopped as Brett reached up to grab Skull's mount's bridle and saw the sapling roped to the scout's back to keep him upright. He felt a cold shaft surge through him; there was blood on the man's buckskin shirt and his face. 'What's happened, Harve?'

'See for yourself. Skull's dead. Been shot three times, but he's been beat up and worked on beforehand.'

'Meg! Where's Meg?' Hatch yelled frantically pushing through the small crowd now gathering.

'Can't rightly say, Milo,' Harve replied in an unusually mild tone. He fumbled in his shirt and brought out a piece of bloodstained paper that seemed to have been torn from a small notebook. He thrust it towards Brett. 'Was pinned to Skull's shirt.'

There was just enough light for Milo to see the words scrawled through the blood and dirt:

you can see by the skinny one we ain't foolen brett — bring what we want by sunup or yull never recognize the girl — an bee alone.

Andy Stein and Chuck Iles steadied Milo Hatch, who was speechless, mouth hanging open. 'What — what's this mean?' he stammered at last.

'Means I gotta go into them canyons and try to bring your daughter back alive,' Brett said quietly. Suddenly he was the focus of everyone's attention.

Lindeen stepped up, took the note and read it. 'You know what they want?'

187

Brett nodded. 'And you can give it to them?'

Brett shook his head. Milo let out a strangled cry and lunged for him, but Harve stepped in between tham and restrained Hatch, glaring at Brett.

'I heard the shots, I think. When we were fixin' them spoiled brands. They couldn't be too deep in the canyons or I wouldn'ta heard anythin'.'

Brett nodded his thanks for the information, checking his six-gun now.

'You can't go alone,' Lindeen said.

'Anyone else tries to come and is sighted, they'll kill Meg.' Brett paused, glancing briefly at Milo. 'Or at least do . . . something to her.'

Milo struggled again. 'I'm coming! You can't stop me! She's my daughter and — '

Brett hit him with the gun barrel, knocking the man senseless. Harve caught Hatch as his knees buckled.

'I go alone. I see anyone trying to follow me, I'll shoot him out of the saddle.'

When, a little later, he rode out into the thickening darkness, watched by the silent trail men, Harve Ricketts muttered:

'He's up to somethin'! Doesn't want anyone else hornin' in. Now I wonder why that is . . . ?'

'Wonder all you like, Harve,' Lindeen told him, making the foreman jump — he hadn't realized anyone had heard him. 'But you try to go after him and I'll shoot you myself. You'll only endanger the girl. Her safety's the most important thing now.'

Says who? Harve wanted to grind out a curse but clamped his mouth hard and strode away, thinking angrily:

So Brett's gonna be the hero! If the son of a bitch lives through it!

* * *

Tad Ripley's mistake was in setting the time limit at sunup.

It gave Brett all the hours of darkness to find the outlaw camp and figure out what was to be done.

He had already made up his mind that if the girl had been violated — or killed — then he would kill Ripley and the rest — every last one of them . . .

He might damn well do it anyway.

She was just a kid, feisty, spoiled, bordering on the arrogant, but she was still growing up. And he wouldn't live easy if Ripley cut her young life short. Ripley wouldn't live at all . . . but he had to remember Yank and Boots and Dutchy. They were all hardened outlaws, saw little more than the dollar signs in anything — or anyone.

And they paid for whatever prosperity they found with bullets.

No use trying to evade the issue: the only way to handle this was to go in with the set decision that he was going to *have* to kill them all — and the girl would be right smack in the middle of it.

He'd had easier problems to solve . . .

But first, he had to find the outlaws' camp.

★　★　★

'Leave her be or I'll shoot your pecker off and mebbe that'll make you think of somethin' else!'

Yank whirled, down on one knee where the girl lay bound hand and foot on a crude bed of branches. She watched him with wary but defiant eyes, feeling his hands drop away from unbuttoning her torn shirt.

'Aw, I was just gonna have a peek, Tad,' he squawked.

'Go right ahead, Yank — if you figure it's worth dyin' for.'

Yank Bilby swallowed as Ripley thumbed back his Colt's hammer. 'Hell! Why we go to the trouble of gettin' somethin' like — *this*! — an' just leave her lie there?'

'Because she's bait, you dumb Yankee. She's gonna bring Brett to us. He spots her and sees she been damaged by you — or anyone else . . . ' he glared at Boots and Dutchy, 'he either won't come in, or he'll come like a cavalry charge.'

'He's only one man,' Dutchy pointed out.

'How long you know him?'

'Well, I din' act'lly *know* him. Seen him a few times an' heard about him plenty — '

'Remember *what* you heard?'

Dutchy pursed his lips, tugged at an earlobe and nodded slowly. 'Hell-bender.'

'Hell on two feet! I want him in here where we can jump him. Once he's hogtied, we can work on him and find out where he stashed the money — ' Tad swept a cold look around at the other three. '*Then* you can have your fun — with him or the gal. Or both.'

'She'll yell out if she sees him,' warned Boots.

'Gag her.'

'When?'

'When it gets closer to sunup.'

'Hell! He'll be lookin' long before then.' Even as he spoke, Boots glanced around at the darkness beyond the small fire and the camp area. He licked his lips briefly.

'Shoulda made the time limit midnight or somethin',' Dutchy said quietly.

'How good you see in the dark? You

part cat, mebbe?'

'No, but waitin' to see him is OK, but s'pose he finds us before then?'

Ripley smiled crookedly. 'Yeah, just s'pose he does — and *if* he does, he's gonna see the gal's pretty much unharmed. So he'll come up like an Injun to get her outta the way first, safe an' sound, before he comes for us.'

Dutchy shifted uneasily. 'That's a lot of guesswork, Tad.'

'I've knowed him since the war. He wasn't much more'n a kid then, pretty wild, homeless, no kin still livin'. They put him up for a medal of honour but he walked away from it.'

'Judas! Why?'

Ripley shrugged, hesitating. 'I — dunno. Said he didn't see any honour in killin' men the way he'd had to, somethin' like that. It was what he was expected to do and he done it, so he figured that was that. Let it lie.'

'Yeah,' Yank said, nodding slowly. 'He always was a mite queer when it come to killin'.'

Boots Skene was still looking in to the darkness beyond the fire glow. 'Reckon we ought to have someone up on that ledge, Tad. I don't like the notion of Brett lyin' out there with his rifle an' pickin' us off one by one.'

'After the first shot he'd come in,' Ripley said confidently, looking at the girl and her big eyes. 'When he sees what'll happen to her if he don't.'

Someone of the other three swallowed loudly. Another cleared his throat. Ripley smiled thinly.

'Draw straws, boys. Short one gets the grandstand view from the ledge.'

Yank Bilby was the 'lucky' one, but no one would ever have known it from the way he cussed out Boots for suggesting the vigil in the first place.

12

Deal or Die!

It was too easy, way too easy.

Brett dismounted just inside the entrance to the block of canyons, holding the bridle of the sorrel, feeling for its ears and finding them twitching as the animal checked things out to its satisfaction.

But they paused twice — moving in the same general direction. He stood ready to clamp a hand over the sorrel's muzzle, but there was no sound from the horse except its breathing.

Brett walked warily in the direction in which the horse had shown an interest, loosening his Colt in its holster. There was a drift of coarse sand underfoot here that deadened the sound of his progress and the horse seemed content to follow easily.

Several times he stopped, stood close to the sorrels head, feeling the slight tension in the neck now when the head moved. There was the suggestion of a snort and he quickly clapped a hand over the muzzle. The animal shook its head with annoyance and he held his breath, hoping it wouldn't whinny its displeasure. It just shook its head once more and stomped a forefoot as a warning.

Tension tightening all his muscles now, Brett mounted, leaned forward to pat the sweaty neck, speaking softly. When he felt the ear stiffen and steady he heeled the mount in that direction at a slow pace.

The land began to rise and he loosened the rifle in its scabbard, surprised to find his palm a trifle sweaty. He let the horse have its head up the slope and then reined in sharply just as they topped out on the rise.

Something blinked below and to the left, just for a moment, perhaps as his gaze passed between two trees, or even between the leaves of a bush. It could have been a firefly — or a spark.

Or a small campfire.

He eased out of the saddle again and, leading the horse with one hand, the other holding his rifle, Brett made his way along the top of the rise, moving until he could see past a clump of trees and — there it was, towards the rear of a hollow. A small campfire.

There wasn't much light shed by the fire but he could make out a couple of shadows that might have been bedrolls. He looked around cautiously, every nerve alert now — and the sorrel whinnied. It startled him so that he jumped slightly and felt his heart do a somersault as his hand tightened on the rifle.

At the same time, a second, unseen horse answered and he heard the crunch of a boot on crumbling sand stone, almost directly above, on a large boulder. *Guard, Distract him with the fire while the guard nails him* . . .

Brett lowered the reins, felt quickly

about and found a head-sized rock which he worked across the ends with his boot. He watched the dim outline of the boulder above, saw something move across the stars, briefly blotting them out from right to left.

He rolled in quickly against the rock's base as a gun above him triggered. The flash briefly lit the rockface and the ground around him, and he glimpsed a tall shape above, leaning out slightly as he worked the rifle lever for a second shot.

Brett spun on to his back, his rifle coming up and firing. The lever worked instantly and the snarl of the first bullet ricocheting still hung in the air as he fired again. The man triggered, too, and the lead drove into the earth a foot from Brett's shoulder.

Then a body thudded to the ground almost beside him, a rifle clattering down a few seconds later. Brett crouched now, Winchester ready, angled up, willing the echoes of the gunfire to clear from his ringing ears.

There were no night sounds now, no insects, no mournful wails of night predators or swooping birds on the hunt for dark-loving rodents. The only sounds he was really aware of was his steadying breathing through his nostrils and the thudding of his heart. He didn't even hear a sound from the sorrel.

He waited, a hunch telling him not to make another move just yet. He thought maybe there had been two guards, but then a voice hailed from below:

'Yank! You get him?'

That was Boots Skene.

'Yank . . . ?'

Brett's mind was racing. But that second naming of the guard he had just killed caused him to take his chances — he saw no other way.

He cleared his throat a little, raised his voice to almost a falsetto, in a not very good imitation of Yank Bilby's high tones. Maybe they'd allow for his excitement at just having survived a gunfight — or he could be wounded . . .

'Got him. Comin' in.' He gasped the words.

A brief silence, then, 'He better be still alive.'

That was Tad Ripley. Brett swore, not wanting to try to imitate Yank again but now having no choice.

'He's OK. I'm hit.' He slurred the words hoping it would help make them believe it was Yank talking.

'Bring him down an' we'll tend to both of you.'

Brett grunted and hoped it would be taken for an affirmative: his throat was already aching from straining in the high reaches.

Now — how the hell was he going to get down there without getting his head shot off?

It was a foregone conclusion that they would be waiting with guns cocked and itchy trigger fingers.

One thing about Ripley, he might have been reckless in some of the jobs they'd pulled, but, by hell, he didn't take any chances when his own life might be endangered.

Neither did Brett McCabe.

★   ★   ★

'How about I go see what the hell's takin' him so long, Tad?' Boots Skene asked, fingering his rifle.

'No. He's comin'. I can hear a hoss now — two. One leadin', most likely.'

'Yank sounded hurt,' added Dutchy worriedly from where he crouched several feet from the others.

'Long as Brett's alive enough to talk.'

Dutchy frowned: so this was how Ripley thought. The sooner he quit this group, the better — preferably with pockets bulging with gold.

'There!' Boots said suddenly, voice tight. 'I seen somethin' — left of the trail comin' down. You got it, Tad?'

'Uh-huh.' Ripley was studying the vague movement. Looked like Yank was leading a second horse with a body draped over it. 'By hell, if that stupid

Yank's killed Brett he's gonna be right behind him when he goes through the gates of Hell.' He whirled as Dutchy moved. 'Stay put! Let 'em get into the camp before we show ourselves.'

He glanced towards the left where the girl lay half in deep shadow, bound *and* gagged now. He had placed her so that anyone entering the camp would see her — they wouldn't see that he had his gun trained on her, but someone like Brett would figure that.

Mebbe Yank had told the truth: Brett was wounded and out of commission — but Tad Ripley would wait to make sure.

The moving shadows began to take on substance and Tad heard the others' sighs of relief. Yank was in the saddle of the lead horse, head down, one hand with the reins wrapped around the wrist, the other hand holding a lead-rope which ran to Brett's sorrel a few feet behind.

Brett's body hung over the saddle, arms trailing, hat hanging and held on only by the tie-thong caught around his jaw and one ear. Nice touch.

Ripley released his own sigh of relief: Brett posed no danger draped in that position. But, by hell he looked *dead*!

'Yank! If you've killed Brett, I'll — '

'He can't hear you, Tad!'

Brett's voice froze all three and Ripley at last saw that Yank was held in the saddle by a sapling roped to his back, just the way he had sent Skull back to Lindeen.

'Watch out!'

By that time, Brett was off the horse, had slapped the lead-rope free and was crouched with six-gun blazing, shooting at the sound of Ripley's voice.

But the outlaw leader was fast as a snake, already rolling down the slope behind his hiding place, sliding to within feet of where the girl lay. He glimpsed her wide eyes above the gag as she struggled frantically and futilely against her bonds. Crouching, he ran towards her.

Guns were blasting the night slightly

above him and he ducked instinctively as he crashed down beside Meg Hatch.

'Just relax, sweetie. You an' me are gonna be a lot closer before this night's finished!' Ripley chuckled as he wriggled in against her.

Brett was lying full length now, shooting beneath the sorrel as it reared and whinnied. He rose in one lunging, fluid movement, snatched his rifle from the scabbard as the horse started to run after Yank Bilby's mount, the dead man bouncing and falling to one side, but still roped to the saddle. The horse with its grotesque rider disappeared into the trees and brush, the sorrel following, but slowing.

Boots Skene was making whining noises as he cursed Ripley for being so sure that Yank had really wounded Brett. He crouched within the tree line, reared up, triggering his rifle in a fast volley. Bullets chewed bark and sap from the young trees, tore through tops of brush, leaves spinning in a cascade.

'*This* time you won't be playin'

possum, you son of a bitch!'

Then Brett's rifle cracked twice, very rapidly. Boots sort of jumped to his feet, body shaking with the strike of the bullets, trying desperately to lift his smoking gun. Brett's third shot took him through the middle of the face and Boots crumpled.

Before he hit the ground, Dutchy was shooting desperately at the muzzle flashes of Brett's Winchester. One of his slugs chewed a handful of splinters from the tree near Brett's face and he swung away, clawing. Dutchy's other bullets made a deal of noise passing through the brush.

Blinking, Brett dropped to the ground, wiping at his prickling cheeks with his upper right arm. Dutchy panicked when he saw the rifle muzzle tracking him, fired one wild shot, then started to run.

He took maybe seven steps before the last two bullets in Brett's magazine cut him down in mid-stride.

Crumpling his neckerchief, Brett

wiped savagely around his right eye, feeling minute splinters pricking like the fuzz on cactus fruit. He blinked rapidly, making the eye water, made sure he changed to a clean corner of the neckerchief, one that hadn't picked up any splinters, and dabbed.

He could see better but not as clearly as he wanted.

There was movement at the rear of the camp and — the girl was gone.

He had seen her lying there before he had ridden in behind Yank, faking his condition by lying across the sorrel. That was why he had come in at an angle so that any shooting would be away from Meg.

As there was no sign of Ripley, it didn't take a genius to realize the man had taken the girl with him as a hostage — or more likely, knowing Ripley, as a body-shield.

He heard a horse, to his right and above the hollow, lifting to a fast run, and in seconds he wheeled to look for the sorrel. It was standing in the tree line now, ears rigid and alert, watching him. He ran towards it and it instinctively started to move away. But a few gasping words settled the animal long enough for him to snatch the reins. Then he was in the saddle, spurring away from the camp with its dead men sprawled untidily around.

Gripping with his knees, swaying his body as they cleared the last trees, he fumbled and thumbed home cartridges into the rifle's loading gate. He dropped two or three but figured he had at least five in the magazine. When it was in the scabbard he replaced the used shells in his Colt — all by feel, something he had mastered long ago and which had helped keep him alive on several occasions.

There was no sign of Ripley now.

He had gone back into the canyons, the pale rock showing ghostlike as sunup approached. Ripley must know his way around in here and Brett reluctantly stopped. The horse was blowing hard, an almost booming sound overriding anything else he might have been able to hear.

Damn! The only sensible thing to do was to wait until daylight — which wasn't far off . . .

It would be only slightly less dangerous, but this way he could ride into a headshot and never know what hit him.

As he made his decision, Ripley's voice suddenly echoed through the winding sandstone maze.

'Just set there, Brett! You make a fine target against that pool reflectin' the stars! No! Don't move or you know what'll happen to the girl — I'll shoot her a little at a time, start with the toes, then the feet. Got me?'

'Not yet, Tad. But I will.'

Ripley laughed. 'Never! Not ever, you sassy son of a bitch. Hey, Brett? Guess what I'm holdin'?'

'Enjoy while you can, Tad.'

Again that chuckle. Brett couldn't quite pin down the location because of the echoes. Ripley was operating true to form. 'An' that'll be any time I like! It's deal or die time, Brett.'

'What's the deal?'

'Playin' dumb, uh? OK. You want the girl, I want the money: we trade. Simple as that.'

'Can't do it.'

'Don't start that again!'

'I don't have it.'

'Where is it?' Ripley was getting a cold edge to his voice now, agitated.

'Bolan has it.' That brought the stunned silence Brett had hoped for. Then he added, 'I gave it to him to save my neck — a dead man can't spend money, Tad.'

13

Telford

It was a lot of money, thanks to the fact that they had an insider working for the Wells Fargo Express in Telford.

Tad Ripley handled all contact with the man, an old acquaintance, and now a clerk in charge of the schedules. His name was Mort Damon and he was a man in trouble: he owed gambling debts all over town and he had, in his panic, seduced the wife of the chief gambler in the hope that she could buy him a little time. Now the man was on the verge of finding out why his wife was so interested in Damon's welfare.

He needed more time. More time to get out of the territory, but he let the woman — and the gambler — think it was so he could raise the money . . . 'Just another week.'

Then he received the news that a large payroll for the borax mines at Sandoval was due. The company was actually closing down and because of some juggling of shares on the financial market it was essential that part should remain hush-hush.

Mort Damon was a man of many talents and had once ridden the owlhoot trail, right after the war ended, with a wild bunch under the leadership of a now notorious robber and killer, Tad Ripley. Mort, wounded in a hold-up, was abandoned by Ripley, but he managed to survive and figured that one day he would square things with the outlaw; he might even be able to claim the reward on Ripley's gang by divulging what he knew. But Ripley's growing reputation as a ruthless killer had frightened him off that notion.

Then, after the gambler's wife told him she had been unable to buy him more than a few days' extra time, Mort reacted more recklessly than ever. He knew that if he ran blindly he was as good as dead. He needed a plan . . . or help.

Then, figuring that by now he had absolutely nothing to lose, Mort went looking for Tad Ripley at some of the old hideouts he remembered. Amazingly, he found him without having his head blown off and Mort put it to him quite simply:

'For a quarter share I'll tell you all you need to know to grab that Borax payroll: when, where, how much. It'll be more'n twenty thousand, I can guarantee that. It's wind-up money, a pay-out. Could be a big haul.'

The dangled carrot grabbed the interest of Ripley and his gang, of which, at this time, Brett McCabe was a member. Ripley curled his thin lips.

'An' all you're askin' is five thousand, eh?'

'It's worth it to you, Tad. I'll tell you all you need to know. I'm the transit clerk so I have all the times and the routes, number of guards and so on.'

Ripley grinned that tight-lipped smile

of his. 'Mort, ol' son, we could just drag that outta you with a hot brandin' iron and a blunt knife.'

Damon blanched. 'You could. But not *all* you need to know. 'Cause I won't know when it's gonna come, an' how, till a couple days before. You could hit the place blind, and pick up no more'n a few hundred, mebbe not even that — but that's a long ways from twenty thousand minimum, ain't it?'

His heart was pounding and he felt his gorge rise, but he forced himself to stick to his guns now. He felt better when he saw the faces of the unkempt outlaws; they had twenty thousand plus on their minds, not pocket money . . .

So, it was arranged.

Brett didn't like the fact that they had to go into Telford itself and take the money from the Express office. That put them too close to the law and Hank Bolan was noted for being a tough sheriff, able to whip up a posse at the drop of a hat. Brett would rather they held up a stage carrying the strongbox along the trail, where there was a better chance of a getaway. But Damon shook his head.

'They won't send that much by stage; it'll come by train and they'll have plenty of guards. Once they offload it to the Express office, it's our responsibility.'

'And Bolan's?' Brett asked, knowing he voiced a question that was on the others' minds, too.

Damon nodded, tight-lipped. 'Afraid so. But I can leave a duplicate key so you can get in the rear door. Just drop the key in the river when you cross it, afterwards, but smash up the doorlock before you go, so they'll figure you had to force it.'

It appealed to most of the gang; there were six members at that time: Ripley, Yank, Boots, Brett, Stormy Chaplin and a crazy killer named Buzz. They had had a bad run, lately. Brett had been thinking seriously of quitting; he was tired of Ripley and the kind of men he recruited these days. He used to enjoy the raids, the sense of adventure that he had grown to like during the War; even the risk of death or being wounded gave him a boost. But lately Ripley had been too quick on the trigger. People who were no danger to the gang were shot just for the hell of it, cabins burned for no good reason — like guerilla raids during the War. If he could get a decent stake from this job he'd quit, just keep riding, outrun the posses, and see where he ended up.

Damon was a nervous wreck; his time limit for settling his gambling debts was fast approaching and still no word had come about the big payroll. There was even a whisper that the borax company heads were making a run with the profits and abandoning the mine and workers. But that was just stupid conjecture. The company had a fine record with employees and customers and creditors and the pay-out would be made on schedule as promised. He *knew* it!

Word came through at last that the

money would be delivered on the noon train from Socorro. Sheriff Hank Bolan wasn't taking any chances; if someone was loco enough to try to steal the payroll at high noon in Telford itself, then they deserved to die — and die they would, shot down by a dozen of his armed deputies.

But the delivery was made without incident, although a small crowd gathered when word got out that the payroll was worth fifty thousand. The real value was closer to thirty-five thousand which was still considerable and able to attract a lot of attention and wistful dreaming.

Damon passed the word to Ripley and the gang came down out of their hole in the wall. Ripley sent Brett in to the pre-arranged rendezvous to pick up the key which Damon would leave there.

'I trust you, Brett.' Ripley gave him that strange smile. 'Besides, you ain't as well-known as the rest of us.'

'Till now.'

'Aw, we'll be clear of town before they even get a glimpse of us. If the key ain't there, come back to the camp and I'll go see Mr Mort Damon personally.'

The key wasn't there — only a note.

Change of plan. My share now half. Leave a silver dollar here if you agree. Key will be here tomorrow. Last chance before money moved.

Of course, Ripley was furious, as were the others.

'You don't seem surprised,' Ripley snapped at the silent Brett, who shrugged.

'You're dealing with a thief, Tad. No reason to think he's got any more moral values than the rest of us.'

Ripley scowled. 'I hate the way you twist some things, Brett.'

'Look at it this way. Half's better than nothing. And we've come a long way just to turn round and go back with empty pockets because Damon's put you in a snit.'

'The hell with that!' Yank exploded in his piping voice, bringing a few twisted smiles to the faces of the otherwise disgruntled outlaws. 'It'll only cost a silver dollar. We don't have to give the son of a bitch his damn share! Pay him off with a bullet — much cheaper.'

That was the sort of thing Brett didn't like, but the rest of the gang were all for it. The big double-cross would make them all rich beyond their dreams.

'You in, too?' Ripley asked Brett aggressively.

Brett had no feelings about Damon, except he savvied how desperate the man must be to risk making such a move, so he nodded, and the robbery was under way.

But Damon was even more devious than they had figured. Remebering how Ripley had abandoned him once, he decided to turn in the whole gang and collect the reward. A real stand-up citizen.

So, Bolan's posse was waiting in ambush, but for some reason didn't make a move until the gang had gone inside and come out again with the money.

There was no moon, but the stars were bright as lanterns in that wide country where there were no large industries within 300 miles to foul the crisp air.

The gang made good targets as they ran to where the unsuspecting Stormy Chaplin held the getaway mounts. They were pooling the heavy bags of gold coins when Buzz spotted one of the posse men creeping through the trees.

Without hesitation, the killer's gun came up blazing and the deputy went down without a sound, but the crash of gunfire had split the night and Bolan's guns opened up.

Caught flat-footed, the gang scattered to their mounts, bullets slashing through them. Buzz went down, tumbling, clawed at the wound just above his belt on the right side. He bared his teeth as he emptied his Colt at the ambushers in a last act of defiance. A hail of lead set his body jerking and jumping as if someone were pulling strings.

Stormy Chaplin rode his mount in as, left with the sack containing the bags of money, Brett struggled to lift the heavy canvas bag high enough so he could hook the loop on his saddle horn. Maybe Chaplin had no intention of grabbing the loot, maybe he was going to help cover Brett's escape, but his gun was out and throwing down in Brett's direction.

Brett slammed his weight against his horse and sent it sideways, protestingly, into Chaplin's path. Stormy hauled rein, firing at Brett, who palmed up his six-gun and blasted him out of the saddle. A bullet burned across his own saddle with a buzzing sound. He jammed a boot into one stirrup, swung clear of the ground, hanging on to the saddle horn as the horse lunged forward. He was on the side away from the posse, began shooting under his mount's neck. The horse didn't like it, tossed its head, weaved and jerked. The motions probably helped to save Brett as the posse's lead snapped wildly about his rocking figure.

He swung on board fully as they crashed into brush, not knowing — or caring too much — where the rest of the gang were.

He saw Ripley only once, as the man raced into the brush. Damon jumped out with a gun in his hand, acting out his good-citizen role to the limit, or, more likely, making sure Ripley wasn't captured alive. Tad was carrying the sawn-off shotgun, the only one the gang possessed, and he gave Damon one barrel. Mort went down writhing and Ripley twisted in the saddle, slowed down for a deliberate shot, and blew the man's upper body to shreds with the second barrel.

Then Ripley disappeared into the darkness among the trees and that was the last Brett saw of him — until he turned up in this canyon country after escaping from the territorial prison . . .

The gang scattered — every man for himself.

The chase was long and relentless. Brett's horse, weary and staggering, took him into a clump of trees near the edge of the badlands. He was almost falling from the saddle with fatigue. During the last two days he had watched the five posse men who were trying to ride him down drop off one by one as their mounts or their resolve gave out.

But there was one rider who didn't quit — and wouldn't: Sheriff Hank Bolan.

He caught up with the fugitive after Brett misjudged the height of a tree branch. He ducked but it slammed him out of the saddle. He had managed to pull himself upright by the horse's quivering foreleg, blood running down his face from a cut on his head, when Bolan appeared, with rifle cocked.

The lawman was trail-dusted, sweaty, and Brett could smell him but figured he must stink just as bad.

'That bag swingin' on your saddle horn looks kinda heavy, man. Bring it over here.'

Brett was slow in responding, still dazed from his fall. Bolan walked his mount over and cracked him across the shoulders with his rifle barrel. Brett spun instinctively, grabbed the barrel and pulled the startled lawman out of the saddle. He was fumbling to reverse the rifle when Bolan's six-gun whipped out of leather and the sheriff crabbed his way to his feet, eyes narrowed. 'I oughta shoot you!'

Brett shrugged; he was so exhausted, he really didn't care whether he was shot or not.

Then Bolan's next words shocked him fully awake.

'I do that, though, they'll want to know where the money is and I'll have to hand it in.'

Brett frowned, not believing what he was hearing. He held his breath. It could be the last one he ever took.

Bolan must have had some idea of

this all along; the reason why he had trailed and hounded Brett so relentlessly these past few days was because *he wanted the money, not the robber.*

'S'pose I was to turn you loose, Brett.' The lawman grinned mirthlessly as his gun barrel jerked towards the white, pulsating hell of the badlands. 'Let you get away — out there.' He glanced at the heavy sack.

'Get away ... ? A damn lizard couldn't cross those badlands alive.'

Bolan nodded. 'Pretty rough place, all right. Only a really desperate man would make his run out there — *really* desperate, afraid for his life if he didn't, but knowin' there was a big chance he wouldn't make it anyway. Anyone'd figure you'd die out there, Brett. Dozens have. No one'll go lookin', that's for sure. But if they figured you'd died in the badlands, then the money must still be with you — gone for ever.'

Brett didn't care for Bolan's notion but his reasoning was all too correct. No one would ever look for the money again. If by some miracle his body was found in the alkali, they would think he had ditched the heavy bag so as to make better time or to give himself more of a chance to escape. They might search but would never find the money.

'Early retirement?' he asked Bolan and the sheriff's tight grin was answer enough.

But Brett *had* made it across the badlands; how, he had never really understood, except that his black horse had been one of the finest animals he had ever owned — and he ended up having to kill it so as to put it out of its misery.

Staggering on, shouldering his saddle, he had felt there was still a faint chance of making a different life for himself, even without any money — if only he could clear the badlands completely.

Coming across Lindeen in that cave and saving him from the two killers had been the best thing that had happened to him in ten years.

Now it was all about to blow up in his face.

14

Last Man

Now he was back facing Ripley, his Nemesis, it seemed — and all the man wanted was the money. *No, not all: the son of a bitch wanted Brett dead, too.*

'Let me tell you how it was, Tad,' he called, wondering where Ripley was hiding, with the girl still a hostage.

'Tell it how you want me to *believe* it was, you mean!'

'How it *happened*, Tad.' No answer, so he briefly described the last part of the pursuit and Bolan's jumping him and stealing the money. 'He had the drop on me and by then I didn't care what happened to the damn money. Bolan took no chances. He wanted me to be carrying my guns — *if* I was ever found. No guns, and someone would wonder why. So he unloaded them, stowed 'em with the ammo, right down the bottom of my warbag. He'd already tied my hands, but loose enough so I could work free eventually. He fired a couple of shots to speed me on my way, but he needn't've bothered; I wanted out of there pronto. By the time he'd dropped out of sight I was a far piece away, my horse plumb tuckered. Me, too. No use going back; the rest of the posse would've caught up with Bolan by then. I eventually got my hands loose, loaded my guns, and, with a lot of dumb luck, I made it across.'

Silence . . . dragging on . . .

'Tad?' Brett called, ready to make his move if the chance offered. 'You hear that . . . ?'

'I'm still here — so's the gal. Man she's a ripe one, ain't she?' He added slowly: 'I winged Bolan in the shoot-out when he nabbed us. I guess he faked it up some, made it a good excuse for him to turn in his badge and retire. Gone to California or somewheres, I guess — *with my money*, son of a bitch!'

'Glad you believe me, Tad.'

'Well, it's likely gospel, knowin' you, but it ain't gonna do you any good now — nor the gal.'

There was a tense edge to the words and Brett threw himself sideways, Colt in hand as he rolled. Bullets spat dirt and stones around him; he slid down a small incline, landed in a few inches of cold water at the edge of the pool that had reflected him. A bullet made a strange scraping sound as it ricocheted from the bottom of the pool before bursting through the surface again into the fast-fading darkness. Brett clung to the incline, worked his way along to his right. Ripley fired again, to the left, but was calming down after his first hot-headed reaction, searching for a target now.

'I've still got the gal!' he warned loudly.

Brett continued moving, out of the water and virtually soundless in his progress as he left the hollow and found himself looking through young trees towards a rock ledge where two figures were. One crouched, the other lay huddled but struggling. Ripley leaned back and casually batted Meg across the face with his left hand. Then he lifted slightly from his crouched position, craning to look for Brett.

The girl suddenly swung up her bound legs and kicked out, her riding boots taking Ripley in the middle of the back. He let out a yell as he was slammed forward, well past the point of balance, and tumbled down into the hollow.

Brett leapt up on to the ledge and sprawled headlong as Ripley savagely raked it with rapid gunfire. The outlaw dropped his empty rifle, struggled to get up, lifting his six-gun. Brett fired two deliberate shots over the edge.

Ripley shuddered, half-turned, Colt blasting, but his bullet going wide. He twisted back and Brett shot him again. The bullet knocked him flat, head and shoulders in the shallow edge of the pool. He struggled, gagging as he tried to keep his head above water, gun submerged now. Blood flooded over the man's chin and onto his shirt front.

'That — really gospel — about — Bolan?'

Brett could feel the girl behind him, still fighting her bonds, and said quietly, 'You'll never know, Tad.'

Ripley tried to curse him but his last breath deteriorated into a death rattle.

Brett bolstered his gun and turned to free the girl. He had removed her gag and untied her hands when a horse clattered into the hollow below.

'How you doin', Brett?' called Harve Ricketts. 'Time for you an' me to have a talk, I reckon.'

'You could've stepped in earlier, Harve.'

'You were doin' all right. Had quite a life, ridin' the owlhoot with Ripley, by the sound of things.' He laughed. 'These canyons sure do throw the words when a man's talkin' loud, don't they!'

Brett frowned; so Harve Ricketts had heard him telling Ripley about the sheriff — and it amounted to an admission that he had taken part in the Telford robbery.

'There'll be a big bounty on Ripley after the jailbreak. You want to claim it, Harve?'

Harve laughed again. 'Yeah, thought of that — and them other three bodies back there.'

'You're gonna be rich, Harve.'

'Don't I know it. 'Course, there's bound to be a decent sorta bounty on you, too.'

Brett nodded slowly: that was what he had been afraid of . . . Harve just had to spoil everything by being greedy.

''Dead or alive', Brett?'

'You're a fool, Harve. You'll have to kill the girl, too. Can you do it?'

'Sure. And I'll take my time . . . Get it?'

Meg gasped and clutched convulsively at Brett's arm, his gun arm. He reached to pull her hand free and —

Ricketts had been sitting his horse side-on, his right arm out of sight because of the way he held his body.

Now that arm lifted with blurring speed and the Colt he held roared.

The girl gave a small cry as Brett staggered, crashing into the rock beside her. He went down on to one knee as Harve triggered again and the bullet ricocheted, spraying Meg with rock chips. She swiftly covered her face with her hands, heard Brett's Colt blast three fast shots — all he had left in the gun. They were followed by a grunt and the crash of a body falling. She opened her fingers and looked down to where Harve Ricketts was sprawled on his face, unmoving, a rivulet of blood trickling from under his body.

Then Brett fell, jamming her against the rock, his blood soaking through her shirt.

★ ★ ★

The wagon jolted and brought the pain surging through him again. He groaned and grabbed at the side shelf where they had laid him out, a blanket

232

covering him. He felt the firmness of bandages around his chest.

'Sorry, Meg, rough trail,' a deep voice said up front.

The sun on the canopy glowed a dirty amber. Its heat radiated through the interior — and showed him Meg Hatch sitting on a pile of gunnysacks beside him. He tried a smile but it seemed like too much effort. She reached forward and touched his face with gentle, cool fingers.

'It's all right, Brett.'

He heard the lowing of cattle, the *ching* of spurs and harness beyond the wagon. 'The herd?'

His voice sounded thin and weak to him. It was an effort to speak. He saw the relief on her freckled face.

'Mr Lindeen cut the bullet out yesterday. It had gouged your skin rather than penetrating deeply. Doesn't seem to've done much damage.'

'I — ain't sure I — agree with — that.'

She laughed softly. 'It's really not too

serious. But you should rest now.'

He started to say he was hungry but found himself drifting away . . .

It was dark next time he awoke and a lantern burned dully in the wagon, which was now stationary. He was surprised to see Milo Hatch sitting on the gunnysacks. The rancher nodded curtly.

'I don't like you, Brett, but I want to thank you for what you did for Meg.'

It was coming back more clearly now and Brett tapped the bandages. 'She's already thanked me.'

'I said *I* want to thank you.' He spoke testily, like the rancher Brett recalled. 'Now I guess I've done it.'

Surprised, Brett merely stared. Hatch growled something, stood and stepped down over the tailboard of the wagon, calling, 'Charley! He's awake.'

Lindeen appeared, leaned on the tailboard, looking at Brett. 'Glad to see you so chipper. Meg told me what happened out there in the canyons. I wouldn't worry about shooting Harve.

He was a damn good cowman but not much of a man, I'm afraid.'

'What happened to Ripley and the others?'

'We buried 'em. Too far to take 'em into Bensonville and Casmeier to claim a reward. Hope that doesn't mess up any plans you had in that direction?'

'I never was much on collecting bounties. 'Specially from someone like Casmeier. Likely because there's one on me.' He was a little short of breath. 'I figure by now Casmeier will know all about it. He was suspicious of me. He'd have been looking through his dodgers all this time.'

'I — see. I'll need to make some sort of report about Ripley and his friends. I mean, the whole crew knows there was a shoot-out and men died.'

'Rustlers.'

'Wha — ? Oh, yes, of course, the same ones who stampeded the herd trying to steal our cows.' Lindeen nodded. 'But even so, there's still your worry that the sheriff may have found a wanted dodger with your picture.'

'It's been bothering me some. It's a few years old but I guess he could still recognize me. How far are we from the railhead?'

'Four or five days' drive — if we don't strike bad weather. Or any more bad men.'

'I think I'll be fit enough to ride in that time.'

'Oh, now, don't be foolish, Brett! You were lucky with that wound, but you can't risk it opening up again.'

'Put me on the drag.' When Lindeen snapped his head up, frowning, Brett added, 'It's an easy chore and no one'll wonder about me riding there. Lots of dust, all the action well forward and on the wings. I'd be last man riding. I could slip away any time and not even be missed till sundown.'

Lindeen was silent, digesting this. 'I don't want to lose you, Brett. Apart from still feeling obligated to you. I like your style, the way you stick to your own code. I can't say that about many of the men I've met in my lifetime.'

'You've more'n repaid me for anything you figure I did for you.'

'You won't change your mind?'

Brett shook his head. 'Don't want to do it, but Casmeier's a damn hard horse when it comes to pushing law.'

'You'll need money. I haven't enough cash to pay you for the work you've done.'

'Fifty dollars'll be fine.'

'Good God, man, that's nowhere near enough!'

They argued briefly and a few days later Brett told Lindeen it was time to go: he'd drop off the drag when they reached the dustbowl ahead. The rancher gave him a package containing $130.

'Still not enough,' Lindeen said, shaking hands solemnly. 'Luck, Brett. The best.'

That afternoon, as he rode in the dust of the drag, feeling the ache in his wound but trying to ignore it, Meg Hatch rode out of the haze and ranged her mount alongside.

'Damn Lindeen!'

She smiled a little. 'I'd've been mighty angry if he hadn't warned me you're planning to leave.' He said nothing and she seemed a little disappointed.

'Mr Lindeen and I both owe you our lives, Brett. You know he has a place for you anytime you want to come back?'

'He told me.'

She sighed. 'You're not going to tell me a thing about your plans, are you?'

'Don't want you involved. Casmeier's the kind will come down hard on any one helping me.'

She nodded slowly. 'I see. And I thank you, but . . . ' She paused, not sure if she should say what was in her mind — or if she *could* say it. 'Will you . . . write me when you're . . . safe? Let me know the name you're using, what you're doing and so on? I'd like to stay in touch — very much.'

Then she realized that he had dropped back, slowly disappearing into the rolling dust, even as she spoke.

Oh, God! Had he heard her . . . ?

She waved, hoping he could still see her, then turned back to the herd which stretched for more than a mile ahead of her. She wiped a gloved hand across her eyes, hesitated, and glanced behind one more time.

But the last man riding had already disappeared from sight. Her shoulders slumped.

Then a faint voice reached her: 'I'll write.'

We do hope that you have enjoyed
reading this large print book.
Did you know that all of our titles
are available for purchase?
We publish a wide range of high
quality large print books including:
Romances, Mysteries, Classics
General Fiction
Non Fiction and Westerns

Special interest titles available in
large print are:
The Little Oxford Dictionary
Music Book, Song Book
Hymn Book, Service Book

Also available from us courtesy of
Oxford University Press:
Young Readers' Dictionary
(large print edition)
Young Readers' Thesaurus
(large print edition)

For further information or a free
brochure, please contact us at:
Ulverscroft Large Print Books Ltd.,
The Green, Bradgate Road, Anstey,
Leicester, LE7 7FU, England.
Tel: (00 44) 0116 236 4325
Fax: (00 44) 0116 234 0205

YUMA BREAKOUT

Jeff Sadler

Horseless and down to his last dollar, out-of-work cowpuncher Nahum Crabtree ended up in the small town of Rios. After a spell in jail, he thought his fortunes had improved when a freighting outfit took him on, especially when one of his bosses turned out to be an attractive young woman. Yes, everything was going well — until he became unwittingly involved in springing a convict from Yuma Penitentiary. And that was only the beginning of his troubles . . .

LIGHTNING AT THE HANGING TREE

Mark Falcon

Mike Clancey was the name inside the rider's watch, but many people during his travels called him Lightning. He was too late to stop a hanging, the men were far away when he reached the lonely swinging figure of a middle-aged man. Then a youth rode up and Lightning found out that the hanged man was his father. So why had he been hanged? Soon the two were to ride together in a pitiless search for the killers.